Junior Great Books

5

BOOK TWO

Junior Great Books®

5

BOOK TWO

Family
Humility
Compassion

JERRY ROSS ELEMENTARY
11319 RANDOLPH STREET
CROWN POINT, IN 46307

Great
Books
Foundation

ISBN 978-1-939014-77-1

4 6 8 9 7 5 3

Printed in the United States of America

Published and distributed by

THE GREAT BOOKS FOUNDATION

A nonprofit educational organization

233 North Michigan Ave, Suite 420

Chicago, IL 60601

www.greatbooks.org

Manufactured by Thomson-Shore, Dexter, MI (USA); RMA238HC16, July, 2018

Contents

Humility

Compassion

INTRODUCTION

Welcome to Book Two of Junior Great Books! Here are some reminders about what to expect as you use **Shared Inquiry**™—a way of reading and discussing great stories to explore what they mean.

How Shared Inquiry Works

You will begin by reading along as the story is read aloud. The group then shares questions about the story. Some questions will be answered right away, while others will be saved for the discussion or other activities.

After sharing questions, everyone reads the story again. During the second reading, you will do activities that help you think more deeply about specific parts of the story.

You will then develop your ideas about the story even more in **Shared Inquiry discussion**.

What Shared Inquiry Discussion Looks Like

Your teacher will start the discussion with an **interpretive question**—a question that has more than one good answer that can be supported with evidence from the story. In Shared Inquiry discussion, the goal is not to find the "right answer," but to work together to explore many different answers. Your teacher will ask more questions during the discussion to help everyone think deeply and explain their ideas.

In the discussion, you will give your answer to the interpretive question and back it up with evidence from the story. You will also tell your classmates what you think about their answers and ask them questions to learn more about their ideas.

Depending on the ideas you hear, you may add to or change your original answer to the question. When the discussion is over, people will have different answers to the interpretive question, but everyone will have evidence for those answers and will understand the story better.

Sometimes the class may work on projects after discussion that are related to the story, like writing, making art, or doing research.

You may find that even after the class has finished working on a story, you are still thinking about it. The characters and events in a story may help you think about your own life and the world around you in new ways, or they might bring up a subject you are interested in.

Every time you practice Shared Inquiry activities like asking questions, rereading, and discussing stories, you become a stronger reader and thinker.

Dos and Don'ts in Discussion

DO

Let other people talk, and listen to what they say.

DON'T

Talk while other people are talking.

DO

Share your ideas about the story. You may have an idea no one else has thought of.

DON'T

Be afraid to say what you're thinking about the story.

DO

Be polite when you disagree with someone.

DON'T

Get angry when someone disagrees with you.

DO

Pay attention to the person who is talking.

DON'T

Do things that make it hard for people to pay attention.

Shared Inquiry Discussion Guidelines

Following these guidelines in Shared Inquiry discussion will help everyone share ideas about the story and learn from one another.

1 Listen to or read the story twice before the discussion.

2 Discuss only the story that everyone has read.

3 Support your ideas with evidence from the story.

4 Listen to other people's ideas. You may agree or disagree with someone's answer, or ask a question about it.

5 Expect the teacher to only ask questions.

Asking Follow-Up Questions

In Junior Great Books, the teacher isn't the only person who can ask questions. *You* can also ask questions if a classmate says something you want to know more about or understand better. These kinds of questions are called **follow-up questions.**

To ask good follow-up questions, you need to really **listen to what your classmates are saying**. When you listen closely, you will hear details that you may want to hear more about. On the next page are some examples of questions you might ask during a discussion or other Junior Great Books activities.

Remember:

- **You can also agree and disagree with your classmates**. Speak directly to them instead of only talking to the teacher, and explain why you agree or disagree.
- **A follow-up question is a compliment**. When you ask a follow-up question, you show that you are listening to and thinking about what others are saying. When someone asks you a question, they are interested in your ideas.

Things you might hear from your classmates:	**Follow-up questions you might ask:**
Words or phrases that you don't quite understand	"What do you mean?" "Can you say that again?"
An idea you want to know more about	"Can you say more about that?" "Why do you think that?"
An idea that needs to be backed up with evidence from the story	"What part of the story made you think that?" "Where does that happen in the story?"

Theme Introduction

Family

In this section of the book, you will read about characters' relationships with their families. Thinking about these stories, and about your own experiences, will give you new ideas about what it means to be part of a family.

Important Questions to Think About

Before starting this section, think about your own experiences with family:

- Do you feel your family understands you? Why or why not?
- Can you think of a time when you had a conflict with someone in your family? How did you find a solution?

Once you have thought about your own experiences with family, think about this **theme question** and write down your answers or share them aloud:

What should family members be expected to do for one another?

After reading each story in this section, ask yourself the theme question again. You may have some new ideas you want to add.

I'm neck and neck with Kip.

KAMAU'S FINISH

Muthoni Muchemi

"Wooyay, please with sugarcane juice," I silently pray. "Let me be one of the lucky ones today." Although Kenyatta Primary Academy in Nairobi has almost four hundred students, not many parents have showed up for Sports Day. I don't care about other parents so long as Baba is there for me.

While the headmistress screeches something or other on the squeaky microphone, I scan the group standing on the other side of the track. Baba is not among them. He's tall and big like Meja Rhino the champion wrestler, so you can't miss him.

My team is the Red House, and we're squashed between the Yellow and Blue House teams. Immediately across is the three-step winners' podium. I cross my eyes three times in its direction, shooting lucky *uganga* rays.

But Chris and Daudi pull my T-shirt and break my concentration. I bat their hands away and crouch down. We're sitting on the ground right in front of the track. Mr. Juma, our sports master, let us sit here because we helped him mark the track into lanes with white chalk. Murram dust will fly in our face during the races, but we'll still have the best view.

Suddenly I see a tall figure approaching from a distance and shoot up again. But Baba is half bald, and this man has tight clumps that look like sleeping safari ants scattered about his head.

"Down, Kamau!" barks Mr. Juma.

My race will start in a few minutes. I close my eyes and slowly mouth the secret word. *Ndigidigimazlpixkarumbeta!* Please let Baba be here by the end of this blink. But I open my eyes too soon, way too soon.

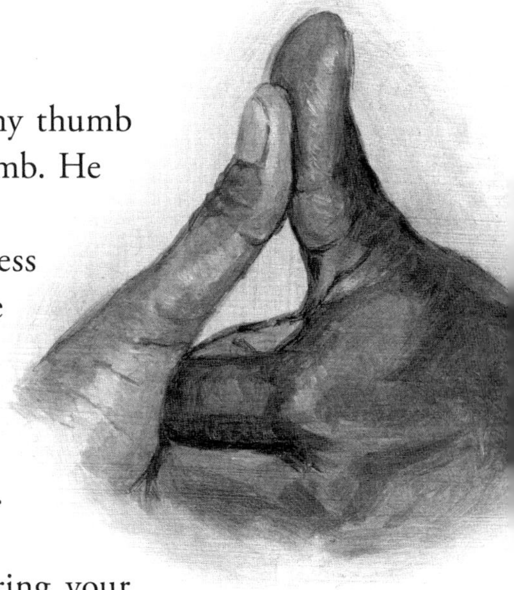

Still, I will not lose faith.

Just this morning, I pressed my thumb into the fleshy pad of Baba's thumb. He didn't pull away.

"I have an important business meeting, Kamau, so we'll just have to see." His dark brown eyes seemed full of heavy thoughts.

I pushed my thumb in harder to drill my way into focus. "Please, Baba . . . "

Mami butted in, "Stop pestering your father. Only thinking about yourself. How self-ish can you be?" She is hugely pregnant and can scold until your head vibrates. "Your father has to work. Do you think the money we use to educate you is donated by foreign aid? Maybe you think we can feed on saliva like bacteria, or live on yesterday's skin like fleas? You have no idea about the financial problems—"

Baba coughed. Mami stopped talking, and for a moment they stared at each other. Mami lashed at me again. "What's that mashing thumbs *uganga* anyway?"

My eight-year-old sister, Wanja, laughed, giving us all a good long look at the mushy stuff in her mouth. Neither of my parents said anything about her bad manners. She had just shown them her report card and, as vomit usual, she was first in her class. Of course, they then asked for mine, and I had to dig it out of the bottom of my bag.

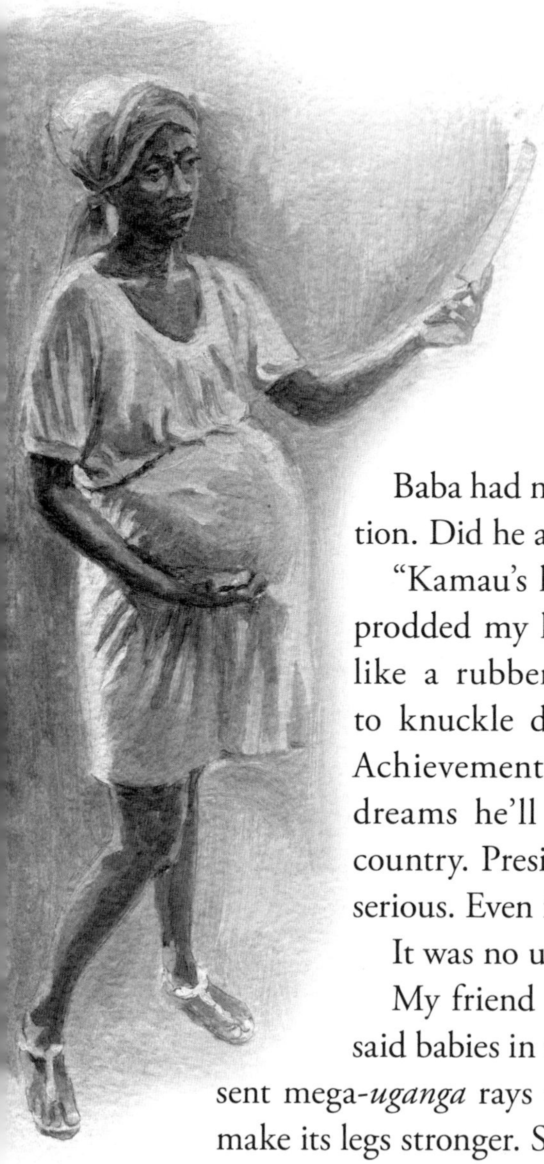

"'Kamau needs to concentrate. He is easily distracted . . .'" Mami had waved the report at Baba. "Didn't I tell you that all this boy does night and day is dream? If they tested a subject called dreaming, Kamau's grades would burst through the ceiling and pierce the cover of the sky!"

Baba had nodded his head in Mami's direction. Did he agree with Mami?

"Kamau's head is full of nonsense!" She'd prodded my head. I let it bob up and down like a rubber ball on a string. "He needs to knuckle down. I want him to succeed. Achievement is what matters. Maybe he dreams he'll be the next president of this country. President Kamau? Heh! Kamau, get serious. Even future kings need to work."

It was no use telling her I try.

My friend Chris once told me his mother said babies in the belly kick. So I squinted and sent mega-*uganga* rays to the baby in Mami's belly to make its legs stronger. She stopped talking and placed a hand over her side.

Maybe my *uganga* rays were too strong.

I held my breath in awe of my powers, but nothing else happened.

Then Njau, my four-year-old brother, had piped up in his high voice, "Baba said effort is what matters."

Baba rumbled, "And problems help us grow."

Mami had scrunched her face as though a mountain of firewood pressed her head and waddled off to pack my special energy lunch—sweet potato slices, *maziwa lala,* boiled egg, two carrots, and an orange.

I bite into the pad of my thumb. It's tingling. *Ndigidigimazlpixkarumbeta!*

"Sit down, Kamau, how many times do I have to tell you?" Mr. Juma's voice rises up and whips me back down.

I glance over at the Yellows and silently chant, "Yellow, yellow, dirty fellow," when my eyes lock with Kip's. He points his index finger and cocks his thumb at me. I duck the imaginary bullet, but he's laughing, trading high-fives with his mates, and doesn't notice. Kip is ten, a year younger than most of my class, and usually the fastest. But twice during practice runs this term, I beat him. He spat at me and sulked off. Everyone else clapped me on the back, even Mr. Juma.

When I told Baba, he said, "Well done, son," and "Good for you."

Now if only Baba would get here, I'd show him how I did it. I'd prove to him that I'm not just a hopeless dreamer.

Our 800-meter race is announced over the screechy microphone. I stare desperately at the parents' side of the track as we file to the starting block. He isn't there.

Three runners from each team stand at attention. Mr. Juma calls for silence.

"Good luck," says Chris in a hoarse voice.

"Same to you," I whisper as we crouch down in starting position.

"On your marks!"

Daudi is in the farthest lane. His lips are moving in silent prayer. Kip calls him *mkiha,* the last carriage of a train. Of course, Kip sees himself as the engine, the one that always gets to its destination first.

I look past Daudi. No sign of Baba, only other parents jostling to get a better view of their sons at the starting line.

Mami said I was selfish to need Baba here today, but I so want to prove to him and Mami that I can be a winner. If he comes just this once, I'll never ask him again.

"Get set!"

I look down at my hands splayed on the ground and feel such a sharp tingling in my thumb that I glance up.

And there he is! My thumb never lies. There is Baba, pushing his way through the throng of parents along

the track. There is no mistaking that huge shining head floating above the rest, hurrying in my direction.

Boom! The gun goes off.

I want to burst with happiness. But a blur of bodies has already bolted forward. They have a head start.

I have to concentrate on the race instead of thinking about the miracle of Baba being here. I glue my eyes on the nearest runner, a blue T-shirt. I concentrate on catching up with him. I run like Ananse the hungry hare on his way to Mr. Elephant's feast. I overtake him.

Concentration, concentration, concentration now begins. To that beat, I run faster. I run in long hard strides that bounce off the ground and pull on the backs of my thighs. My legs feel strong. I set my sights on a yellow back. A surge of warmth floods my body as I overtake him.

I can tell it's Daudi directly in front of me, because he runs with his head facing the sky. He's already slowing. I pound past him with my eyes locked on Kip's yellow shirt.

He's in a cluster, but I know Kip always goes for the flashy sprint finish. I have to catch up with him now if I'm to have a chance. Concentration, concentration, concentration now begins.

Amid all the crowd noises, I think I hear Baba yell, "Run, son!"

A new energy tingles from my feet, up along my legs, loosens my hips, and expands my chest. I tear past Chris, who is panting like a horse. *Uganga* magic is with me!

The cluster is breaking up. Kip is racing ahead. My heart hammers in my ribs. I open my mouth wider to take in more air. I'm catching up. I'm in the dispersing cluster. I overtake one, two, three boys.

I'm flying, my feet almost slapping my bottom, half a step behind Kip.

When I win this race, Mami will never scold me again. When I win this race, Wanja will swallow her snickering. Best of all, Baba will look in my eyes to congratulate me. Baba will finally see me.

Everything feels slow motion. The noise, the people, and the track float away into the great *uganga*-land of dreams. I hear only distant echoes. "Win, win, win!"

I'm neck and neck with Kip, matching him stride for stride. He leans in my direction as though to draw strength from me. The finish-line ribbon flutters red maybe fifty meters ahead.

I'm going to win! I'm going to win! My teammates will carry me on their shoulders, shouting, "Hero! Hero!" When I climb the winner's podium to collect my medal, I won't even punch the air or do a show-off dance. Baba will already know I'm a hero. Baba will—

An unexpected shove jolts me out of my dream and back to the moment. Then I'm wobbling, fighting for control. I fall.

Unbelievable!

I swallow the grit on my tongue and shake my head to clear the ringing in my ears. I feel confused. Not quite on this earth. My hands are grazed with white track chalk mixed with brown soil and smudges of blood. I shape them into fists and press hard to force the pain away. A blue shirt whizzes by, kicking dust in my face.

While I was in my dream, Kip must have pushed me with his elbow. Mami would be proud of a son like Kip, who knows winning is what matters.

Legs zoom past me in a whir of hot air and dust. I glance toward the side of the track. The crowd probably thinks Kip and I touched accidentally.

A cheer goes up and I realize Kip must have crossed the red ribbon. Kip has won my race. No. Kip has stolen my race.

I want to call to Baba that I should have won. Will he believe that Kip tripped me?

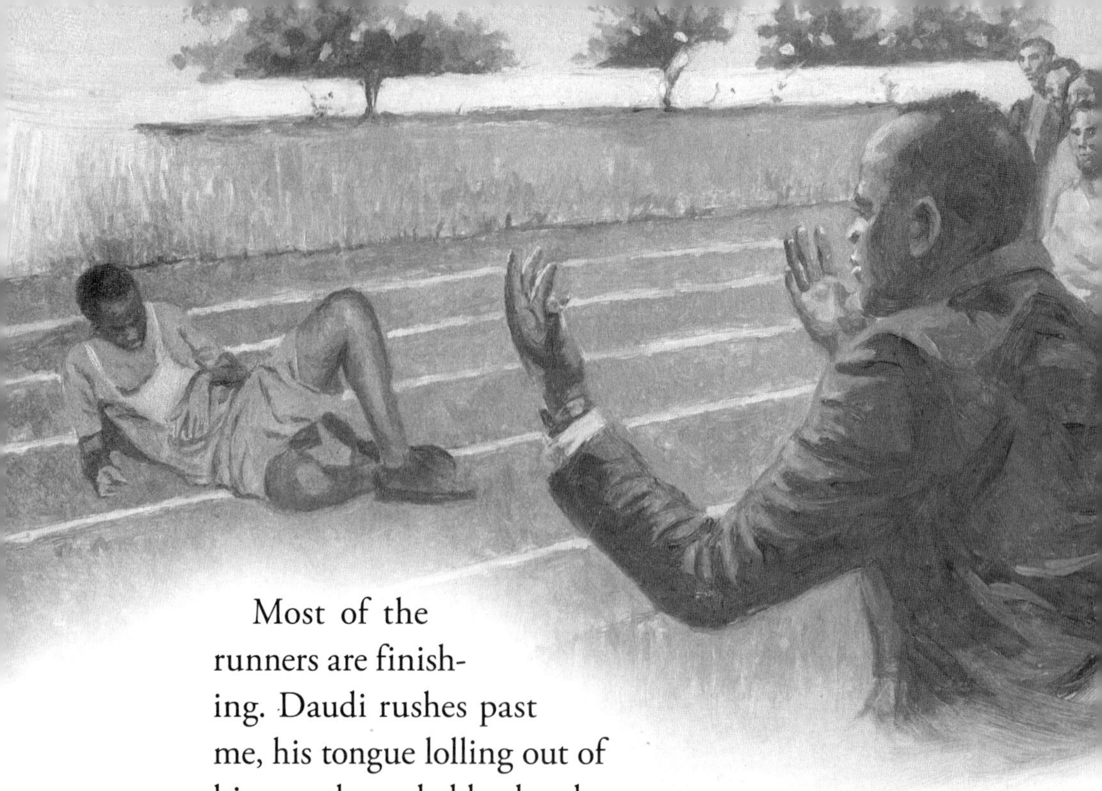

Most of the runners are finishing. Daudi rushes past me, his tongue lolling out of his mouth, probably elated not to be the *mkiha* for once.

I look back and see Baba's shiny face. He is running alongside the track, gesturing wildly—up, up, up—pointing to the finish line. But how will getting up help me? I'll pretend my leg is broken. I'll give a dramatic cry for help. I'll—

I become aware of the noise, the cheering. They're chanting my name. "KA-MA-UU! KA-MA-UU! KA-MA-UU!" They're shouting for me to finish. I feel like shouting back, "Whatever for? All I'm good for is dreaming."

Then I notice their eyes are not on me, but on my lumbering Baba, who has crossed onto the track behind me. He is wearing a black suit and shiny lizard shoes he bought donkey years ago that usually make me cringe.

My ears buzz, but I think I hear him shout, "Run, son! Get up and run!"

Uncertain, I scramble up and gape at Baba. Sweat streams down his face, and he holds a hand over his chest. Is he having a heart attack?

He can't be. His eyes are shining. I can see every tooth in his mouth.

Baba is beaming!

So I wipe my nose with my wrist and laugh through the tears. It sounds like I am crying. But Baba is beaming.

I keep my eyes on him and trot sheepishly alongside to the finish. So much noise, so many people crowding the finish area. Mr. Juma is probably shouting for order.

But I only have ears for Baba.

"Is the cat watching us now?" he whispered.

Ghost Cat

Donna Hill

It was growing so dark that Filmore had to stop reading; but as soon as he put his book down, he began to notice the loneliness again.

His mother had been driving without a word ever since they had turned onto this remote and bumpy road. Jodi was asleep, curled up in back with her stuffed animal friend. There was nothing to see out the window except black trees and shrubs along the roadside thrashing in the wind. To the west, through the trees, he could see that the sun had melted onto the horizon, but to the east the sky looked dark and bruised.

Suddenly his mother said, "That must be the house." She stopped the car.

Jodi sat up. "Are we here?" Jodi always awoke at once, alert and happy. She did not seem to know what loneliness and sorrow were. Jodi had glossy black curls and eyes like agates. She was little for her six years, but sturdy and fearless, as even Filmore would admit, but only to himself. To others, sometimes as a compliment, he said she was daft.

"You two wait here while I take a look," said their mother.

Filmore watched their mother walk along the path between the swaying, overgrown bushes. She looked small, walking alone, not much taller than his sister, in fact. Filmore whispered, "Jodi, don't you wish Daddy were here with us?"

Jodi was brushing down the apron of her animal friend.

"Remember last summer with Daddy?" Filmore said. "The beach, how broad and clean and dazzling it was? Remember what fun we had in the boat?"

Jodi turned her animal friend about, inspecting her from all sides.

"Here comes mother," Filmore said. "Let's not remind her of Daddy." But he needn't have warned Jodi. She seemed not to have heard a word.

"This is it," their mother said. "Help me with the bags, please, Filmore."

He and Jodi scrambled out of the car.

"Wait, wait!" Jodi called. "I dropped Mrs. Tiggy-winkle! Don't worry, Mrs. Tiggy-winkle! We'll never leave you! We love you!"

"What does she care," Filmore protested. For some reason he was annoyed with his sister. "She's only a stuffed hedgehog."

"She is not! She's a raccoon!"

"Listen, either she's a hedgehog or she's not Mrs. Tiggy-winkle!"

"Filmore, please," their mother said, pushing through the creaking gate.

A stone path led to a cottage perched on a little bluff overlooking the cove. Trees were sighing and moaning over the roof, and shrubs whispered at the door. The wind dropped suddenly as though the house were holding its breath, and Filmore could hear the push of waves up the beach and their scraping retreat over pebbles and shells.

His mother paused at the stoop to search through her bag for the key. Now Filmore could see scaling paint, shutters hanging loose, and windows opaque with dust. "What a dump!" he muttered.

When he saw his mother's face, he was sorry. His mother had gone back to teaching and labored to keep up their home; no one knew better than Filmore how hard it had been.

"The agent told us we'd have to take it as is," she said. "That's how we can afford it." She found the key, but could hardly shove the door open for sand that had sucked up against it.

"We came for the beach, anyway," Filmore said. "Who cares about the house! I wouldn't care if it was haunted!"

"Oh, I love the haunted house!" Jodi cried, bursting into the front room. "Oh, we have a big window with the whole black sky in it! Oh, and a fireplace! And rocking chairs!" The floor squealed under her feet as she ran around excitedly. "And here's the kitchen, with a black monster stove!"

Their mother laughed. She had the same dark curly hair, the same eyes as Jodi, and when she laughed, she did not look much older. "It's charming, really. Just needs a little work. But first we need some sleep."

They climbed narrow stairs and opened creaking doors to three small rooms with beds under dust covers. The covers pleased their mother and made Jodi laugh. "Ghosts and more ghosts!" she cried.

In his unfamiliar little room above the kitchen, Filmore kept waking in the night to whistles, squeals, and thumps that could have been ghosts in the house, that could have been anything sinister at all.

The next morning, Filmore woke to the melancholy crying of gulls. When he heard Jodi's light voice below, he pulled his clothes on hurriedly and went down to the kitchen.

"Good morning, dear," his mother said from the stove, where she was already cooking breakfast. "Did you sleep well?"

"I didn't sleep at all," Jodi put in cheerfully. "Neither did Mrs. Tiggy-winkle. We stayed awake all night and listened to the haunted house."

Filmore did not want to admit his own feelings. "You're daft!"

"Something is here, you know," Jodi insisted. "Something besides us!"

"And I know what it is." Their mother laughed. "Sand! We'll get rid of it right now."

The house was so small that sweeping and dusting upstairs and down did not take long, and still there was time for the beach before lunch.

To Filmore, the beach was even more disappointing than the house. It was narrow and deserted, with low, dispirited waves the color of mud as far as the eye could see. There were no houses in sight, just cliffs and scraggy pine trees at each end of the cove. Edging the sand were patches of weeds and damp brown rags of algae that

smelled like vinegar. The stain that marked high tide was littered with broken shells, sticks like bones, and here and there a dead fish. A troupe of sandpipers ran up the beach and back, as though frantic to escape.

Jodi loved everything. She made up a joyful beach song as she built a sand dragon and then she pressed Filmore to go with her while she filled her bucket with shells and treasures.

Stumping along at her heels, Filmore demanded, “Why don’t you ever talk about Daddy? You were his dear rabbit, don’t forget!”

“Look, Filmore!” Jodi cried. “I found a sand dollar!”

After lunch, they drove out for supplies. “It will be fun to see the village and the shops,” their mother said.

The village turned out to be only a few houses scattered along the road, and on the beach, one rowboat upside down beside a shack with a sign for bait. The shops were only Judson's General Store and Judson's Gas Station.

A bell jangled as they went into the store. It was dim and cluttered and smelled of dusty bolts of cloth and strong cheese. Behind the counter stood a tall, thin woman who kept her hands in her apron pockets while she looked them over with stern interest.

"Good morning!" their mother said. "I'm Mrs. Coyne. This is my son, Filmore, and my daughter, Jodi. We've rented the Hogarth place."

"Heard you did," said the storekeeper.

"We need milk and a few groceries. Also lumber and nails, if you have them. We'd like to mend the front stoop. You don't think the owner would mind, do you?"

"Not likely. He hasn't seen the place in years. But I'd wait if I were you. See if you like it there, first."

"Don't you think we'll like it?" Filmore asked.

"Been a lot of folks in and out the Hogarth place. City folks, mostly. Like you. They never stay long."

"Because it's rundown, or is there something else?" Filmore asked.

His mother interposed. "Do you happen to know if the chimney works?"

"Did once. Likely needs sweeping."

"Is there someone who might do it for us?"

"Mr. Judson. My husband. He can fix the front stoop, too, if you want. Rehang those shutters. Trim the bushes. You would have to pay, though. The real estate agency won't. Cost you twenty dollars."

"That would be just fine!"

When Mrs. Judson was adding up the prices on a paper bag, Filmore asked, "Why don't people stay long at Hogarth's?"

Mrs. Judson was busy checking her figures.

"Because of what's there besides us," Jodi said. "Isn't that right, Mrs. Judson?"

Their mother looked at Mrs. Judson with a smile, but Mrs. Judson was busy packing groceries.

"But we like it, Mrs. Tiggy-winkle and I. It sounds so beautiful and sad. Especially the little bell."

"What little bell?" Filmore asked.

"Didn't you hear it? It was so sweet last night, going tinkle-clink all around the house."

Mrs. Judson rang up the money with a loud jangle of her register. "Suit you if Mr. Judson comes tomorrow morning?"

Back in the car, Filmore said, "She wasn't very friendly."

"I thought she was," said their mother. "She tried to help us all she could."

"She didn't smile, not once," Filmore said. "And she wouldn't tell us anything."

"That's because she was nervous," Jodi said.

"Why would she be nervous?" their mother asked.

"For us. She thinks we might be afraid in the house."

"But there's nothing to be afraid of!" said their mother.

Jodi laughed. "We know that!"

Early next morning, Mr. Judson arrived in a truck, with toolbox and planks of wood. He too was tall and thin, with the same gaunt face as his wife, but with a tuft of gray beard attached.

All morning while they were on the beach, Filmore could hear Mr. Judson hammering, thumping, and snipping. At noon he came and said, "Chimney's working. I laid a fire. Got to go, now. The missus will be waiting."

They walked with him to his truck. "How do you folks like it here?" he asked, lifting his toolbox into the back.

"We love it!" Jodi answered.

"It's a charming house, really," their mother said. "I wonder why it hasn't been sold?"

"Because of what's here," Jodi said. "Isn't that right, Mr. Judson?"

Mr. Judson was searching among his tools. "Must have left my pliers somewhere, Mrs. Coyne."

"It's a cat," Jodi said.

"A cat, Jodi?" their mother asked. "Are you sure? Is there a cat, Mr. Judson?"

"Never saw one here, myself. Leastwise not in years."

"You mean there used to be a cat?" Filmore asked.

"Mrs. Hogarth, she had one. Hogarth, he moved away when his missus died. Don't know what became of the cat."

"Could it be a neighbor's cat?"

"She has a squeaky little voice," Jodi said. "Probably hoarse from crying."

"Haven't heard tell of any lost cats," Mr. Judson said. He went around to the cab of his truck.

"Could it be a stray?"

"Oh, she's not a stray," Jodi said. "She wears a little rusty bell that goes tinkle-clink when she runs. It's so sweet."

Mr. Judson climbed into his truck and turned on the ignition. "If you find my pliers, will you bring them next time?"

As they watched the truck rattle down the road, Filmore asked, "Don't you think the Judsons act strange? Like they're hiding something?"

"No, dear," his mother said. "I think they're just reticent. That's how people are in this part of the country."

That night, Filmore was awakened by someone shaking his toes. "Filmore! I have to tell you something!"

Jodi was leaning against his bed with Mrs. Tiggy-winkle in her arms. Moonlight falling through the window made her eyes like holes in a mask. "Do you hear the cat?" Jodi whispered. "She's prowling and crying all around the house, now. She wants to come in."

Filmore held his breath to listen. He did in fact hear a wailing and sighing and rustling of leaves. "That's the wind."

"And the cat, too," Jodi insisted.

"All right, get in my bed, if you're scared."

"We're not scared. But we are cold." She climbed on the bed and settled the quilt around Mrs. Tiggy-winkle.

Filmore rolled over and closed his eyes. "Go to sleep. There isn't any cat. Mr. Judson said so."

"He did not. He said he never saw a cat, leastwise not in years. But we did."

Filmore turned back. "You saw it?"

"Yes, on the beach this afternoon. She was watching us through the weeds, a yellow cat with red eyes."

"Then why haven't Mother and I seen it?"

"Because she's invisible."

"You said you saw it!"

"We did! Mrs. Tiggy-winkle and I! Both of us! First we saw her eyes and then we saw her whole self!"

"You don't even know what invisible means!"

"We do too! It means mostly people can't see her."

"It means nobody ever sees her!"

"But she can fix that when she wants to. Anyway, she is prowling and crying right now. She wants somebody to let her in."

"If she's invisible, she can let herself in!" Filmore cried, triumphantly.

"That's not the same," Jodi said, straightening the quilt.

Filmore turned away. "You make me tired! What did you come bothering me for!"

Jodi sighed and threw off the covers.

"You can stay if you're nervous," Filmore muttered.

"We aren't nervous. But you are! So we'll stay."

At breakfast, Jodi said, through a mouthful of blueberry pancakes, "When you have a cat, you're her mother and daddy, you know, so you must never leave her, like Mr. Hogarth did. That's why she's always crying and prowling and never can rest."

Their mother looked down at them from her pancake griddle.

"We have to put some food out for her, Mother," Jodi said.

"If there's any cat around here, it finds its own food," Filmore said.

"That's right, dear. It got along all right before we came."

"No, she didn't! She's skinny all over and her little bones show! Can't I give her my milk? Please, Mother, please!"

Their mother smiled. "Not your milk, Jodi. We'll find some scraps."

Filmore followed Jodi to the kitchen stoop, where she settled the scraps and a pan of water.

"She's already been here, looking for food," Jodi said. "See her paw prints?"

Filmore bent to examine the stoop. "That's just wet sand. The wind did that. You're putting this food here for nothing. No cat's going to eat it."

"Of course not. She's a ghost. Ghosts can't eat."

"Then why are you putting it here!" Filmore exclaimed, exasperated.

"She doesn't need to eat it, just to have it. To know we love her."

On the beach that afternoon, their mother was reading under the umbrella while Jodi sat beside her on the sand, sorting her beach treasure. Filmore waded for a while, but he felt uneasy by himself and soon came back to flop beside his sister.

The grasses above the beach rattled in the wind. "Is the cat watching us now?" he whispered.

"Oh, not now. The hot sand hurts her feet."

"I thought you said she was a ghost!"

"But she can hurt, just the same."

Later, clouds rolled up over the sea and the wind turned cold. Filmore took down the umbrella while his mother folded the beach chair and they ran for the house through pellets of rain.

That evening Filmore forgot the cat in the pleasure of popping corn over a snappy fire. Their mother sat rocking and mending, and Jodi sprawled on the hearth, humming to Mrs. Tiggy-winkle. Firelight threw quivering shadows on the walls. Outside the rain was like handfuls of sand thrown at the windows.

Filmore glanced at his mother. Her face was thoughtful and withdrawn. Whenever he caught her in such a mood, she would quickly smile, as though to insist she was all right. This time, however, she spoke.

"Remember last summer? Our last vacation with Daddy? Remember the day he bought every balloon the man had, and you three went along the beach and gave them away to children? He wanted us to share our happiness. Remember, Jodi, how happy he wanted us to be?"

"Is it popcorn yet?" Jodi asked. "I don't hear any more pops."

When Filmore passed her the popcorn, she said, "Mrs. Tiggy-winkle feels just the same as me. But not the cat. She hurts. Because she was murdered. That's why she's a ghost."

Filmore saw that his mother's needle had stopped, but she did not look at them.

"When somebody leaves you, they always murder you a little bit. But Mr. Hogarth, he murdered her a lot, until she was dead."

"If you know so much, how did he do it?" Filmore demanded.

"First he starved her and then he drowned her and then he told her she was bad. That's why she's so skinny and wet. She hates to be skinny and wet. She's outside now, crying at the kitchen door. Can't you hear her? She wants to come in by the fire."

"You're daft!" Filmore exclaimed. "That's just the wind!"

"Please, Mother, please! Can't I let her in?"

Their mother gave Filmore a glance that asked for patience. "All right, dear. Let her in."

Jodi rose with Mrs. Tiggy-winkle and went to the kitchen. Filmore heard the kitchen door open and then the screen. A cold draft blew through the room and dashed at the flames on the hearth.

"Hurry up, please!" their mother called. "You're cooling off the house."

When Jodi came back, Filmore said, "Well, where is the cat?"

"She can't come in because she knows you don't love her."

"But you and Mrs. Tiggy-winkle love her! Isn't that enough?"

"Can Mrs. Tiggy-winkle have some more popcorn, please?"

When the fire burned low and their mother announced bedtime, Jodi said, "She's crying again, Mother."

"Jodi, dear, why do you upset yourself this way? Can't you just enjoy your vacation with Filmore and me?"

"Yes, but she has to be happy, too! That's why we came here, you know! Can't I let her sleep on my bed tonight?"

Their mother sighed.

"You think I just imagine her, don't you?"

"Of course!" Filmore said. "You are the only one who sees her!"

"I am not! Mrs. Tiggy-winkle sees her, too!"

"And Mrs. Tiggy-winkle isn't real, either!"

"All right, if I just imagine her, why can't I have her on my bed?"

Their mother smiled. "I can't argue with that."

In his room, Filmore heard the squeal and slap of the screen door and then his sister's clumpy steps on the stairs. Straining, he thought he also heard soft paws running up beside her and the tinkle of a bell.

"Now she's got me doing it!" he muttered.

The rain grew quiet, the wind died, waves gently washed the shore. The next time Filmore opened his eyes, it was nearly daylight. He pulled on his robe and went to his mother's room.

"What is it, Filmore?" she asked. Like Jodi, she always woke up at once.

"Let's see if Jodi really has a cat."

He took her hand as they went down the hall. "You don't believe there's a ghost cat, do you?"

His mother stopped in the hall. "Not literally, dear, of course. But Jodi does, so we must try to be understanding. She's still very little, you know. She isn't quite sure where reality stops and the stories of her mind begin."

"But why would she make up this crazy story?"

"We'll have to see if we can think of why."

Jodi's window opened on a huge dark sea and a rosy horizon. The sound of rolling waves was like the breathing of a giant in sleep. Jodi was curled under the quilt, her black hair shining on the pillow and Mrs. Tiggywinkle under her chin.

"There's no cat!" Filmore whispered. "She made the whole thing up!" He felt an odd mixture of indignation, relief, and disappointment.

Jodi sat up brightly. "We're not asleep!"

"Did you and Mrs. Tiggy-winkle have a good night?" their mother asked.

"Yes, and so did the ghost cat. She stayed right here on my bed till she got warm and dry, and then she went away."

To Filmore she added, "If you don't believe me, look at this! She gave me her bell!"

Jodi opened her hand to show him a little rusty bell on a bit of frayed ribbon.

Filmore was going to accuse her of finding the bell on the beach, when he caught his mother's eye.

"Why did the ghost cat leave you?" their mother asked. "Doesn't she love you?"

"Yes, but she had to go because she was dead. Just like Daddy, you know."

Filmore saw his mother's eyes grow cloudy, but she hid them by hugging Jodi. He went and made a circle with them, turning his face away also.

Muffled by their arms, Jodi said, "That's why we're hugging and crying and smiling, right?"

The wet park was glittering all around him.

THE HEMULEN WHO LOVED SILENCE

Tove Jansson

Once upon a time there was a hemulen who worked in a pleasure ground, which doesn't necessarily mean having a lot of fun. The hemulen's job was to punch holes in tickets, so that people wouldn't have fun more than once, and such a job is quite enough to make anyone sad if you have to do it all your life.

The hemulen punched and punched, and while punching he used to dream of the things he would do when he got his pension at last.

In case someone doesn't know what a pension is, it means that you can do what you like in all the peace you wish for, when you're old enough. At least that was how the hemulen's relatives had explained it to him.

He had terribly many relatives, a great lot of enormous, rollicking, talkative hemulens who went about slapping each others' backs and bursting into gigantic laughs.

They were joint owners of the pleasure ground, and in their spare time they blew the trombone or threw the hammer, told funny stories, and frightened people generally. But they did it all with the best of intentions.

The hemulen himself didn't own anything because he was on the sideline, which means only half a relative, and as he never could put his foot down about anything to anyone he always had to do the babysitting, to work the big bellows of the merry-go-round, and, most of the time, to punch tickets.

"You're lonely and have nothing to do," the other hemulens used to tell him in their friendly way. "So it might cheer you up a bit to lend a hand and be among people."

"But I'm never lonely," the hemulen tried to explain. "I can't find the time to be. There's always such a lot of people who want to cheer me up. If you don't mind, I'd like so much to . . ."

"Splendid," the relatives said and slapped his back. "That's the thing. Never lonely, always on the go."

The hemulen punched along, dreaming about a great wonderful silent loneliness, and hoped he would grow old as soon as possible.

The whirligigs whirled, the trombones trumpeted, gaffsies and whompers and mymbles shrieked in the roller coaster every night. Edward the Booble won a first prize in china smashing, and all around the sad and dreamy hemulen people danced and whooped, laughed and quarreled, and ate and drank, and by and by the hemulen grew simply afraid of noisy people who were enjoying themselves.

He used to sleep in the hemulen children's dormitory, that was bright and nice in the daytime, and at night when the kiddies awoke and cried he comforted them with a barrel organ.

The rest of his spare time he lent a hand anywhere it was needed in a large house full of hemulens, and so he had company around the clock, and everybody was in high spirits and told him all about everything they thought and did and planned to do. Only they never gave him time to reply properly.

"Won't I grow old soon?" the hemulen once asked at dinner.

"Old? You?" his uncle shouted. "Far from it. Buck up, buck up, nobody's older than he feels."

"But I feel really old," the hemulen said hopefully.

"Pish, posh," the uncle said. "We're going to have an extra spot of fireworks tonight, and the brass band will play until sunrise."

But the fireworks never were touched off, because that same afternoon a great rain started to fall. It continued all night and all the next day, and the next one after that, and then all the following week.

To tell the truth, this rain kept up for eight weeks without a stop. No one had ever seen the like.

The pleasure ground lost its colors, shrunk, and withered away like a flower. It paled and rusted, and then it slowly started to disperse, because it was built on sand.

The roller coaster railway caved in with a sigh, and the merry-go-rounds went slowly turning around in large gray pools and puddles, until they were swept off, faintly tinkling, by the new rivers that were formed by the rain. All small kiddies, toffles and woodies and whompers and mymbles, and so forth, were standing days on end with their snouts pressed to the windowpanes, looking at their July becoming drenched and their color and music floating away.

The House of Mirrors came crashing down in millions of wet splinters, and pink drenched paper roses from the Miracle Garden went bobbing off in hundreds over the fields. Over it all rose the wailing chorus of the kiddies.

They were driving their parents to desperation, because they hadn't a single thing to do except grieve over the lost pleasure ground.

Streamers and empty balloons were drooping from the trees, the Happy House was filled with mud, and the three-headed alligator swam off to the sea. He left two of his heads behind him, because they had been glued on.

The hemulens took it all as a splendid joke. They stood at their windows, laughing and pointing and slapping backs, and shouted:

"Look! There goes the curtain to the Arabian Nights! The dancing floor has come loose! There's five black bats from the Cave of Horror on the fillyjonk's roof! Did you ever!"

They decided in the best of spirits to start a skating rink instead, when the water froze, of course—and they tried to comfort the hemulen by promising him the ticket-punching job again as soon as they could get things going.

"No," the hemulen suddenly said. "No, no, no. I don't want to. I want my pension. I want to do what I feel like doing, and I want to be absolutely alone in some silent place."

"But my dear nephew," one of his uncles said with enormous astonishment, "do you mean what you say?"

"I do," said the hemulen. "Every word of it."

"But why haven't you told us before?" the perplexed relatives asked him. "We've always believed that you've enjoyed yourself."

"I never dared tell you," the hemulen admitted.

At this they all laughed again and thought it terribly funny that the hemulen had had to do things he disliked all his life, only because he hadn't been able to put his foot down.

"Well, now, what *do* you want to do?" his maternal aunt asked cheerfully.

"I'd like to build myself a doll's house," the hemulen whispered. "The most beautiful doll's house in the world, with lots and lots of rooms, and all of them silent and solemn and empty."

Now the hemulens laughed so hard that they had to sit down. They gave each other enormous nudges and shouted, "A doll's house! Did you hear that! He said a doll's house!" and then they laughed themselves into tears and told him:

"Little dear, by all means do exactly as you like! You can have grandma's big park, very probably it's silent as a grave nowadays. That's the very place for you to rummage about in and play to your heart's content. Good luck to you, and hope you like it!"

"Thanks," the hemulen said, feeling a little shrunken inwardly. "I know you've always wished me well."

His dream about the doll's house with the calm and beautiful rooms vanished; the hemulens had laughed it to pieces. But it really was no fault of theirs. They would have felt sincerely sorry if anyone had told them that they had spoiled something for the hemulen. And it's a risky thing to talk about one's most secret dreams a bit too early.

The hemulen went along to grandma's old park that was now his own. He had the key in his pocket.

The park had been closed and never used since grandma had set fire to her house with fireworks and moved elsewhere with all her family.

That was long ago, and the hemulen was even a little uncertain about the way to the park.

The wood had grown, and ways and paths were underwater. While he was splashing along, the rain stopped as suddenly as it had started eight weeks ago.

But the hemulen didn't notice it. He was wholly occupied with grieving over his lost dream and with feeling sorry because he didn't want to build a doll's house anymore.

Now he could see the park wall. A little of it had tumbled down, but it was still quite a high wall. The single gate was rusty and very hard to unlock.

The hemulen went in and locked the gate behind him. Suddenly he forgot about the doll's house. It was the first time in his life that he had opened a door of his own and shut it behind him. He was home. He didn't live in someone else's house.

The rain clouds were slowly drifting away and the sun came out. The wet park was steaming and glittering all around him. It was green and unworried. No one had cut or trimmed or swept it for a very, very long time. Trees were reaching branches down to the ground, bushes were climbing the trees and crisscrossing, and in the luscious grass tinkled the brooks that grandma had led through the park in her time. They didn't take care of the watering any longer, they took care only of themselves, but many of the little bridges were still standing even if the garden paths had disappeared.

The hemulen threw himself headlong into the green, friendly silence, he made capers in it, he wallowed in it, and he felt younger than he ever had before.

Oh, how wonderful to be old and pensioned at last, he thought. How much I like my relatives! And now I needn't even think of them.

He went wading through the long, sparkling grass, he threw his arms around the trees, and finally he went to sleep in the sunshine in a clearing in the middle of the park. It was the place where grandma's house had been. Her great fireworks parties were finished long ago. Young trees were coming up all around him, and in grandma's bedroom grew an enormous rosebush with a thousand red hips.

Night fell, lots of large stars came out, and the hemulen loved his park all the better. It was wide and mysterious, one could lose one's way in it and still be at home.

He wandered about for hours.

He found grandma's old fruit orchard where apples and pears lay strewn in the grass, and for a moment he thought, What a pity. I can't eat half of them. One ought to . . . And then he forgot the thought, enchanted by the loneliness of the silence.

He was the owner of the moonlight on the ground, he fell in love with the most beautiful of the trees, he made wreaths of leaves and hung them around his neck. During this first night he hardly had the heart to sleep at all.

In the morning the hemulen heard a tinkle from the old bell that still hung by the gate. He felt worried. Someone was outside and wanted to come in, someone wanted something from him. Silently he crept in under the bushes along the wall and waited without a word. The bell jangled again. The hemulen craned his neck and saw a very small whomper waiting outside the gate.

"Go away," the hemulen called anxiously. "This is private ground. I live here."

"I know," the small whomper replied. "The hemulens sent me here with some dinner for you."

"Oh, I see, that was kind of them," the hemulen replied willingly. He unlocked the gate and took the basket from the whomper. Then he shut the gate again. The whomper remained where he was for a while but didn't say anything.

"And how are you getting on?" the hemulen asked impatiently. He stood fidgeting and longed to be back in his park again.

"Badly," the whomper replied honestly. "We're in a bad way all of us. We who are small. We've got no pleasure ground anymore. We're just grieving."

"Oh," the hemulen said, staring at his feet. He didn't want to be asked to think of dreary things, but he was so accustomed to listening that he couldn't go away either.

"You must be grieving, too," the whomper said with compassion. "You used to punch the tickets. But if one was very small and ragged and dirty you punched beside it. And we could use it two or three times."

"My eyesight wasn't so good," the hemulen explained. "They're waiting for you at home, aren't they?"

The whomper nodded but stayed on. He came close to the gate and thrust his snout through it. "I must tell you," he whispered. "We've got a secret."

The hemulen made a gesture of fright, because he disliked other people's secrets and confidences. But the whomper continued excitedly:

"We've rescued nearly all of it. We keep it in the filly-jonk's barn. You can't believe how much we've worked. Rescued and rescued. We stole out at nights in the rain and pulled things out of the water and down from the trees and dried them and repaired them, and now it's nearly right!"

"What is?" asked the hemulen.

"The pleasure ground of course!" the whomper cried. "Or as much of it as we could find, all the pieces there were left! Splendid, isn't it! Perhaps the hemulens will put it together again for us, and then you can come back and punch the tickets."

"Oh," the hemulen mumbled and put the basket on the ground.

"Fine, what! That made you blink," the whomper said, laughed, waved his hand, and was off.

Next morning the hemulen was anxiously waiting by the gate, and when the whomper came with the dinner basket he called at once:

"Well? What did they say?"

"They didn't want to," the whomper said dejectedly. "They want to run a skating rink instead. And most of us go to sleep in winter, and anyway, where'd we get skates from . . ."

"That's too bad," the hemulen said, feeling quite relieved.

The whomper didn't reply, he was so disappointed. He just put down the basket and turned back.

Poor children, the hemulen thought for a moment. Well, well. And then he started to plan the leaf hut he was going to build on grandma's ruins.

The hemulen worked at his building all day and enjoyed himself tremendously. He stopped only when it was too dark to see anything, and then he went to sleep, tired and contented, and slept late the next morning.

When he went to the gate to fetch his food the whomper had been there already. On the basket lid he found a letter signed by several kiddies. "Dear pleasure puncher," the hemulen read. "You can have all of it because you are all right, and perhaps you will let us play with you sometime because we like you."

The hemulen didn't understand a word, but a horrible suspicion began burrowing in his stomach.

Then he saw. Outside the gate the kiddies had heaped all the things they had rescued from the pleasure ground. It was a lot. Most of it was broken and tattered and wrongly reassembled, and all of it looked strange. It was a lost and miscellaneous collection of boards, canvas, wire, paper, and rusty iron. It was looking sadly and unexpectantly at the hemulen, and he looked back in a panic.

Then he fled into his park and started on his leaf hut again.

He worked and worked, but nothing went quite right. His thoughts were elsewhere, and suddenly the roof came down and the hut laid itself flat on the ground.

No, said the hemulen. I don't want to. I've only just learned to say no. I'm pensioned. I do what I like. Nothing else.

He said these things several times over, more and more menacingly. Then he rose to his feet, walked through the park, unlocked the gate, and began to pull all the blessed junk and scrap inside.

The kiddies were sitting perched on the high wall around the hemulen's park. They resembled gray sparrows but were quite silent.

At times someone whispered, "What's he doing now?"

"Hush," said another. "He doesn't like to talk."

The hemulen had hung some lanterns and paper roses in the trees and turned all broken and ragged parts out of sight. Now he was assembling something that had once been a merry-go-round. The parts did not fit together very well, and half of them seemed to be missing.

"It's no use," he shouted crossly. "Can't you see? It's just a lot of scrap and nothing else! No!! I won't have any help from you."

A murmur of encouragement and sympathy was carried down from the wall, but not a word was heard.

The hemulen started to make the merry-go-round into a kind of house instead. He put the horses in the grass and the swans in the brook, turned the rest upside down, and worked with his hair on end. Doll's house! he thought bitterly. What it all comes to in the end is a

lot of tinsel and gewgaws on a dustheap, and a noise and racket like it's been all my life. . . .

Then he looked up and shouted:

"What are you staring at? Run along to the hemulens and tell them I don't want any dinner tomorrow! Instead they might send me nails and a hammer and candles and ropes and some two-inch battens, and they'd better be quick about it."

The kiddies laughed and ran off.

"Didn't we tell him," the hemulens cried and slapped each other's backs. "He has to have something to do. The poor little thing's longing for his pleasure ground."

And they sent him twice what he had asked for and, furthermore, food for a week, and ten yards of red velvet, gold and silver paper in rolls, and a barrel organ just in case.

"No," said the hemulen. "No music box. Nothing that makes a noise."

"Of course not," the kiddies said and kept the barrel organ outside.

The hemulen worked, built, and constructed. And while building he began to like the job, rather against his will. High in the trees thousands of mirror glass splinters glittered, swaying with the branches in the winds. In the treetops the hemulen made little benches and soft nests where people could sit and have a drink of juice without being observed, or just sleep. And from the strong branches hung the swings.

The roller coaster railway was difficult. It had to be only a third of its former size, because so many parts were missing. But the hemulen comforted himself with the thought that no one could be frightened enough to scream in it now. And from the last stretch one was dumped in the brook, which is great fun to most people.

But still the railway was a bit too much for the hemulen to struggle with single-handed. When he had got one side right the other side fell down, and at last he shouted, very crossly:

"Lend me a hand, someone! I can't do ten things at once all alone."

The kiddies jumped down from the wall and came running.

After this they built it jointly, and the hemulens sent them such lots of food that the kiddies were able to stay all day in the park.

In the evening they went home, but by sunrise they stood waiting at the gate. One morning they had brought along the alligator on a string.

"Are you sure he'll keep quiet?" the hemulen asked suspiciously.

"Quite sure," the whomper replied. "He won't say a word. He's so quiet and friendly now that he's got rid of his other heads."

One day the fillyjonk's son found the boa constrictor in the porcelain stove. As it behaved nicely it was immediately brought along to grandma's park.

Everybody collected strange things for the hemulen's pleasure ground, or simply sent him cakes, kettles, window curtains, toffee, or whatever. It became a fad to send along presents with the kiddies in the mornings, and the hemulen accepted everything that didn't make a noise.

But he let no one inside the wall, except the kiddies.

The park grew more and more fantastic. In the middle of it the hemulen lived in the merry-go-round house. It was gaudy and lopsided, resembling most of all a large toffee paper bag that somebody had crumpled up and thrown away.

Inside it grew the rosebush with all the red hips.

And one beautiful, mild evening all was finished. It was definitely finished, and for one moment the sadness of completion overtook the hemulen.

They had lighted the lanterns and stood looking at their work.

Mirror glass, silver, and gold gleamed in the great dark trees; everything was ready and waiting—the ponds, the boats, the tunnels, the switchback, the juice stand, the swings, the dart boards, the trees for climbing, the apple boxes . . .

"Here you are," the hemulen said. "Just remember that this is *not* a pleasure ground, it's the Park of Silence."

The kiddies silently threw themselves into the enchantment they had helped to build. But the whomper turned and asked:

"And you won't mind that you've no tickets to punch?"

"No," said the hemulen. "I'd punch the air in any case."

He went into the merry-go-round and lighted the moon from the Miracle House. Then he stretched himself out in the fillyjonk's hammock and lay looking at the stars through a hole in the ceiling.

Outside all was silent. He could hear nothing except the nearest brook and the night wind.

Suddenly the hemulen felt anxious. He sat up, listening hard. Not a sound.

Perhaps they don't have any fun at all, he thought worriedly. Perhaps they're not able to have any fun

without shouting their heads off . . . Perhaps they've gone home?

He took a leap up on Gaffsie's old chest of drawers and thrust his head out of a hole in the wall. No, they hadn't gone home. All the park was rustling and seething with a secret and happy life. He could hear a splash, a giggle, faint thuds and thumps, padding feet

everywhere. They *were* enjoying themselves.

Tomorrow, thought the hemulen, tomorrow I'll tell them they may laugh and possibly even hum a little if they feel like it. But not more than that. Absolutely not.

He climbed down and went back to his hammock. Very soon he was asleep and not worrying over anything.

Outside the wall, by the locked gate, the hemulen's uncle was standing. He looked through the bars but saw very little.

Doesn't sound as if they had much fun, he thought. But then, everyone has to make what he can out of life. And my poor relative always was a bit queer.

He took the barrel organ home with him because he had always loved music.

Theme Introduction

Humility

In this section of the book, you will read about characters who are humble and characters who struggle to be humble. Thinking about these stories, and about your own experiences, will give you new ideas about humility.

Important Questions to Think About

Before starting this section, think about your own experiences with humility:

- Can you think of a time when you showed humility?
- Have you ever had a hard time being humble about something?

Once you have thought about your own experiences with humility, think about this **theme question** and write down your answers or share them aloud:

What does it mean to be humble?

After reading each story in this section, ask yourself the theme question again. You may have some new ideas you want to add.

He quietly sat and enjoyed the world around him.

THE ENCHANTED STICKS

Steven J. Myers

Long ago in Japan, near the city of Kyoto, there was an old man who gathered wood in the forest. He picked up fallen limbs and sticks and traded them to the people of a nearby village for rice and tea.

He lived in a small hut at the edge of the forest by the side of a stream. He caught fish with his bare hands and ate them with his rice. After his evening meal he would sit in his doorway, slowly sip his tea, and quietly enjoy the world around him. He listened to the stream flowing by and the breeze in the leaves of the forest. He smelled the scents of the flowers and grass and fresh water. He felt the air soft and delicate on his skin.

One day when he was out gathering wood a band of twenty robbers jumped out from behind the trees. These robbers were both vicious and fearless. They respected no one and stole and killed without mercy.

The robber chief shouted at the old man and flashed his samurai sword.

The old man bowed in greeting, but showed no fear.

"Do you know who we are?" the robber chief asked.

The old man nodded.

"With this sword I could cut you into a thousand pieces to feed the crows. I could do that and it wouldn't bother me at all."

The old man nodded again.

"Oh, you're too stupid to be afraid!"

The old man bowed once more and smiled.

In the thick forest dark there were only a few shafts of light breaking through from the sky. There was the glint and slashing flash of the robber chief's sword in the rare light. Then, shouting "Hai!" he leaped into the air and with one swift slash he cut off the low limb of a tree. Before it hit the ground, he shouted and slashed so quickly that the limb flew apart in a shower of sticks.

The robber chief laughed and snorted. "Old man, *that* should have been you." And then with a wiggling, waltzing swagger-walk he headed toward Kyoto with his men following in poor and ragged imitation.

The old man gathered up the sticks cut by the robber chief. He took the largest one for a walking stick, and then he tied the rest into a bundle separate from the others because they were green and not much good for kindling.

Walking easily through the forest, slipping between the trees, he started home. Months passed and then one day when the old man was about to make a small fire to heat his tea, he dropped the sticks he was carrying. When he bent down he saw that they had fallen into the shape of the characters that spelled out: *Don't burn us!*

He shook his head and smiled. But when he tried to pick up the sticks, they wiggled in his hands and he dropped them again. And again they arranged themselves to say: *Don't burn us!*

This time he scrunched down to examine them closely. The sticks were from the bundle the robber chief had cut.

There was nothing unusual looking about them. They were just plain sticks. But as soon as the old man tried to pick up one, it wiggled loose and fell back into its place on the ground.

"All right," the old man said, "I won't burn you."

Then the sticks danced about and arranged themselves into a smiling face.

The old man laughed loudly and the sticks danced about. That only made him laugh more and the sticks dance more until the sticks and the old man were rolling around in dancing laughter.

After that the old man and the sticks *talked* every day. He shook the sticks a few times and tossed them into the air. They fell into words or, sometimes, whole sentences.

The old man and the sticks played tic-tac-toe. The old man was always the Os and the sticks were always the Xs. The sticks were good at the game, and the old man was pleased no matter who won.

And they would fence: mock sword fights between the old man and one of the sticks. The stick would dance about in the air, swinging and thrusting like the sword of an invisible samurai while the old man fought back with his walking stick. These carefree contests always ended in all the other sticks joining in to make the fight a wild clicking and light clattering of

wood. And then the old man would fall down and surrender with laughter.

And when the old man hummed a song while he relaxed after his evening meal, the sticks clacked together beating time to the tune. Or on rare nights the sticks would take tufts of grass and strips of rag to dress themselves as dancers, actors, and animals. Then they would act out the legends from the far past. Afterward they danced, a slow formal dance, their makeshift kimonos flowing in soft waves in the moonlight.

And when the old man told a story, the sticks played the characters—the princes, the dragons, the lions, the lost maidens—as little stick figures, while the old man delighted in their dancing grace.

The old man was content with his life except—except that the band of robbers had grown larger and larger until now there were a hundred of them. No one was safe. They even attacked villages—taking food, clothes, anything they wanted. Then they burned the people's homes and escaped into the forest.

The emperor sent an army after them, but the robbers hid among the trees and thick brush. When the army entered the forest, a rain of arrows shot out of the green dark. Then the robbers jumped out with slashing swords and knives. They were so expert with bow and arrow and sword—especially the chief—that they easily scattered the army.

Then a band of eleven samurai—proud and brave and very skilled with sword and bow—went out to hunt down the robbers. But they got lost in the forest and wandered about, so that when they did find the robbers, the robber chief alone easily killed them.

A few months later the robbers boldly arrived at the outskirts of Kyoto itself, where they kidnapped a young maiden just as she was to marry a prince. The robber chief demanded a ransom so large that no one could pay. So he put the young girl in a bamboo cage and hung it from a tree. He gave her a samisen and ordered her to play and sing for him and his men.

She refused.

He told her that was fine with him, but she would only get rice if she sang. "A bird that doesn't sing isn't worth the bird seed," he said.

So she sang, but only sad songs. And all through the forest, people heard her sad music and soft song. But they thought that the robber chief had killed her and that it was only her ghost crying in the trees.

Every evening the old man listened to that song. He felt the sadness that thickened the air and dulled the quality of the light. Each note seemed a separate bird that settled on his skin and sank in to become an ache in his bones. Even the enchanted sticks no longer danced as easily or as lightly.

The old man knew something had to be done—but what? His mind was too clouded, too heavy. A clear stream of action couldn't flow from such a muddied source. So he meditated for three days. He just sat quietly by his hut—eating nothing, doing nothing.

Finally his mind was clear. He would ask the sticks.

He went to the stream for a long, cool drink, then into his hut for the enchanted sticks. He shook them and tossed them into the air.

They said: *You only need a small bundle of us. Follow the maiden's song.*

So he bundled the sticks in a strap, threw them over his shoulder, took his walking stick, and stepped out into the dark, night-tuned forest.

The maiden's music was a thread leading him through the night to the robbers' camp. In a few hours he was at the edge of a lake. Far out in the center he could see an island. By the light of four small fires he could see the shapes and shadows of men. He heard curses and rough voices. Then he saw a bamboo cage swaying from a high limb of a tree. The lovely sad song came from there.

The old man sat down at the edge of the water and waited all through the night. At first one fire was put out, then the second, the third, and finally the last one was only a soft orange-yellow glow. The music stopped. The cage swayed silently. Occasionally sounds of snoring came across the water.

The old man waited until morning. Then, in the early mist, he tossed the sticks into the air. They stuck together as if glued to form a ladder. Taking his walking stick, he climbed to the top. Then the enchanted sticks danced apart to become two tall stilts with the old man, his walking stick over his shoulder, calmly at ease upon them.

He walked out into the lake. The water rose slowly until at its deepest point it came up to his ankles. He paused to stir the water with his stick, rippling his strange reflection. Then he strode toward the island.

Two robbers guarded the island. They were half-asleep. They rubbed their eyes. They yawned. Suddenly one of them saw something move in the mist on the lake. He grabbed the other guard and tried to talk—but he was too frightened.

The second robber yelled, "Ghost! Ghost!" and ran away.

The other robbers, awakened by the screams, came running. The robber on guard jumped up and down and pointed. He still couldn't speak.

The old man continued toward them through the mist. The robbers rubbed their eyes. They thought he was walking on the lake. Some shouted. Others ran for their boats to escape. Others dove into the cold water and tried to swim away.

As the old man got closer to the island, the water became shallow. To the robbers, he appeared to grow taller and taller as he came with his eyes shining in the swirling mist.

The robber chief shouted at his men. He called them cowards. Screaming, "Kill the monster!" he rushed toward the old man.

But now the old man jumped down from his stilts. The sticks fell apart to become a bundle of arrows. He made his strap and walking stick into a bow and shot the enchanted arrows at the robbers. He couldn't miss. If a robber ducked, the arrow would whiz by, stop, and make a sharp turn to return to the target. Arrows curved around trees, jumped over rocks, went underground to pop up behind robbers and hit their bottoms.

Now, all the robbers ran away.

Except for the chief. He stood before the old man and flashed his sword.

The old man stepped forward and raised his walking stick to hit the robber chief.

The robber chief cut the stick in two.

The old man raised both pieces to hit the robber.

The robber slashed quicker than sight—and the 2 sticks were 4.

The old man then raised up 4 pieces to hit the robber.

The robber chief slashed and slashed.

Now the old man had 8 sticks.

The robber slashed.

The old man had 16 sticks.

The robber slashed sixteen times, cutting each stick in two.

The old man hit out with 32 sticks.

The robber, sweat pouring now, slashed thirty-two times.

The old man attacked with 64 sticks.

The robber chief cut those in two.

The old man had 128 sticks.

Now the robber chief was shouting and slashing about in a white-faced frenzy.

The old man attacked with 256 sticks.

The faster the robber chief slashed, the worse it got for him. He shouted "Hai! Hai! Hai!" as he cut and cut.

The old man struck with 512 sticks.

The robber chief was crying now. He was on his knees. Tears, dirt, and sweat covered his face. He tried once more, but his brilliant slashing gave the old man 1,024 sticks to attack with.

The robber fell face-down. Exhausted, he sobbed into the ground.

The old man shook his head, bent down to pick up the robber's sword, and threw it into the deep part of the lake. Then he walked over to the tree with the bamboo cage. He picked up several of his enchanted sticks and made a ladder. He climbed up to help the maiden from her cage. He placed her on his shoulders as he helped her down to the ground. Then he turned his sticks into stilts again. He carried the girl across the lake, where he made the sticks into a bundle. Then he put the girl on his shoulders once more and carried her all the way to her home.

When she told her father and family what had happened, everyone offered rich gifts to the old man.

But he said he only wanted the woods, the stream, and his hut.

The old man returned home, undid his bundle, and dropped

the enchanted sticks. They scattered about, but said nothing. They formed no words, made no pictures. The old man tried again. Still nothing. Once more. No words.

He went to the stream, bent down, and scooped out two fish. He cleaned them and put them on a long stick. He got the bundle of enchanted sticks and arranged them into a tent-shaped pile. He took out his flint and struck it to light a handful of dry grass. He set the sticks on fire and cooked his fish. The fish were delicious and the fire crackled and the embers glowed for a long time.

Then the old man took a glowing stick and wrote on the evening air. With the glowing point he made designs, orange-yellow characters, warm-red profiles of lions, dragons, and fish.

And the old man laughed—as free and easy as a child.

Kaddo sat on the wall by the gate.

KADDO'S WALL

West African folktale as told by Harold Courlander and George Herzog

In the town of Tendella in the Kingdom of Seno, north of the Gulf of Guinea, there was a rich man by the name of Kaddo. His fields spread out on every side of the town. At plowing time hundreds of men and boys hoed up his fields, and then hundreds of women and girls planted his corn seed in the ground for him. His grain bulged in his granary, because each season he harvested far more than he could use. The name of Kaddo was known far and wide throughout the Kingdom of Seno. Travelers who passed through the town carried tales of his wealth far beyond Seno's borders.

One day Kaddo called all of his people in the town of Tendella together for a big meeting in front of his house. They all came, for Kaddo was an important man, and they knew he was going to make an important announcement.

“There’s something that bothers me,” Kaddo said. “I’ve been thinking about it for a long time. I’ve lain awake worrying. I have so much corn in my granary that I don’t know what to do with it.”

The people listened attentively, and thought about Kaddo’s words. Then a man said:

“Some of the people of the town have no corn at all. They are very poor and have nothing. Why don’t you give some of your corn to them?”

Kaddo shook his head and said, “No, that isn’t a very good idea. It doesn’t satisfy me.”

Another man said to Kaddo:

“Well, then, you could lend corn to the people who have had a bad harvest and have no seed for the spring planting. That would be very good for the town and would keep poverty away.”

“No,” Kaddo said, “that’s no solution either.”

"Well, then, why not sell some of your corn and buy cattle instead?" still another man said.

Kaddo shook his head.

"No, it's not very good advice. It's hard for people to advise a rich man with problems like mine."

Many people made suggestions, but nobody's advice suited Kaddo. He thought for a while, and at last he said:

"Send me as many young girls as you can find. I will have them grind the corn for me."

The people went away. They were angry with Kaddo. But the next day they sent a hundred girls to work for him as he had asked. On a hundred grindstones they began to grind Kaddo's corn into flour. All day long they put corn into the grindstones and took flour out. All day long the people of the town heard the sound of the grinding at Kaddo's house. A pile of corn flour began to grow. For seven days and seven nights the girls ground corn without a pause.

When the last grain of corn was ground into flour, Kaddo called the girls together and said:

"Now bring water from the spring. We shall mix it with the corn flour to make mortar out of it."

So the girls brought water in water pots and mixed it with the flour to make a thick mortar. Then Kaddo ordered them to make bricks out of the mortar.

"When the bricks are dry, then I shall make a wall of them around my house," he said.

Word went out that Kaddo was preparing to build a wall of flour around his house, and the people of the town came to his door and protested.

"You can't do a thing like this, it is against humanity!" they said.

"It's not right, people have no right to build walls with food!" a man said.

"Ah, what is right and what is wrong?" Kaddo said. "My right is different from yours, because I am so very rich. So leave me alone."

"Corn is to eat, so that you may keep alive," another said. "It's not meant to taunt those who are less fortunate."

"When people are hungry it is an affront to shut them out with a wall of flour," another man said.

"Stop your complaints," Kaddo said. "The corn is mine. It is my surplus. I can't eat it all. It comes from my own fields. I am rich. What good is it to be rich if you can't do what you want with your own property?"

The people of the town went away, shaking their heads in anger over Kaddo's madness. The hundred girls continued to make bricks of flour, which they dried in the sun. And when the bricks were dry Kaddo had them begin building the wall around his house. They used wet dough for mortar to hold the bricks together, and slowly the wall grew. They stuck cowry shells into the wall to make beautiful designs, and when at last the wall was done, and the last corn flour used up, Kaddo was very proud. He walked back and forth and looked at his wall. He walked around it. He went in and out of the gate. He was very happy.

And now when people came to see him they had to stand by the gate until he asked them to enter. When the workers who plowed and planted for Kaddo wanted to talk to him, Kaddo sat on the wall by the gate and listened to them and gave them orders. And whenever the people of the town wanted his opinion on an important matter he sat on his wall and gave it to them, while they stood and listened.

Things went on like this for a long time. Kaddo enjoyed his reputation as the richest man for miles around. The story of Kaddo's wall went to the farthest parts of the kingdom.

And then one year there was a bad harvest for Kaddo. There wasn't enough rain to grow the corn, and the earth dried up hard and dusty like the road. There wasn't a single ear of corn in all of Kaddo's fields or the fields of his relatives.

The next year it was the same. Kaddo had no seed corn left, so he sold his cattle and horses to buy corn for food and seed for a new planting. He sowed corn again, but the next harvest time it was the same, and there wasn't a single ear of corn on all his fields.

Year after year Kaddo's crops failed. Some of his relatives died of hunger, and others went away to other parts of the Kingdom of Seno, for they had no more seed corn to plant and they couldn't count on Kaddo's help. Kaddo's workers ran away, because he was unable to

feed them. Gradually Kaddo's part of the town became deserted. All that he had left were a young daughter and a mangy donkey.

When his cattle and his money were all gone, Kaddo became very hungry. He scraped away a little bit of the flour wall and ate it. The next day he scraped away more of the flour wall and ate it. The wall got lower and lower. Little by little it disappeared. A day came when the wall was gone, when nothing was left of the elegant structure Kaddo had built around his house, and on which he had used to sit to listen to the people of the town when they came to ask him to lend them a little seed corn.

Then Kaddo realized that if he was to live any longer he must get help from somewhere. He wondered who would help him. Not the people of Tendella, for he had insulted and mistreated them and they would have nothing to do with him. There was only one man he could go to, Sogole, king of the Ganna people, who had the reputation of being very rich and generous.

So Kaddo and his daughter got on the mangy, underfed donkey and rode seven days until they arrived in the land of the Ganna.

Sogole sat before his royal house when Kaddo arrived. He had a soft skin put on the ground next to him for Kaddo to sit upon, and had millet beer brought for the two of them to drink.

"Well, stranger in the land of the Ganna, take a long drink, for you have a long trip behind you if you come from Tendella," Sogole said.

"Thank you, but I can't drink much," Kaddo said.

"Why is that?" Sogole said. "When people are thirsty they drink."

"That is true," Kaddo replied. "But I have been hungry too long, and my stomach is shrunk."

"Well, drink in peace then, because now that you are my guest you won't be hungry. You shall have whatever you need from me."

Kaddo nodded his head solemnly and drank a little of the millet beer.

"And now tell me," Sogole said. "You say you come from the town of Tendella in the Kingdom of Seno? I've heard many tales of that town. The famine came there and drove out many people, because they had no corn left."

"Yes," Kaddo said. "Hard times drove them out, and the corn was all gone."

"But tell me, there was a rich and powerful man in Tendella named Kaddo, wasn't there? What ever happened to him? Is he still alive?"

"Yes, he is still alive," Kaddo said.

"A fabulous man, this Kaddo," Sogole said. "They say he built a wall of flour around his house out of his surplus crops, and when he talked to his people he sat on the wall by his gate. Is this true?"

"Yes, it is true," Kaddo said sadly.

"Does he still have as many cattle as he used to?" Sogole asked.

"No, they are all gone."

"It is an unhappy thing for a man who owned so much to come to so little," Sogole said. "But doesn't he have many servants and workers still?"

"His workers and servants are all gone," Kaddo said. "Of all his great household he has only one daughter left. The rest went away because there was no money and no food."

Sogole looked melancholy.

"Ah, what is a rich man when his cattle are gone and his servants have left him? But tell me, what happened to the wall of flour that he built around his house?"

"He ate the wall," Kaddo said. "Each day he scraped a little of the flour from the wall, until it was all gone."

"A strange story," Sogole said. "But such is life."

And he thought quietly for a while about the way life goes for people sometimes, and then he asked:

"And were you, by any chance, one of Kaddo's family?"

"Indeed I was one of Kaddo's family. Once I was rich. Once I had more cattle than I could count. Once I had many cornfields. Once I had hundreds of workers cultivating my crops. Once I had a bursting granary. Once I was Kaddo, the great personage of Tendella."

"What! You yourself are Kaddo?"

"Yes, once I was proud and lordly, and now I sit in rags begging for help."

"What can I do for you?" Sogole asked.

"I have nothing left now. Give me some seed corn, so that I can go back and plant my fields again."

"Take what you need," Sogole said. He ordered his servants to bring bags of corn and to load them on Kaddo's donkey. Kaddo thanked him humbly, and he and his daughter started their return trip to Tendella.

They traveled for seven days. On the way Kaddo became very hungry. He hadn't seen so much corn for a long time as he was bringing back from the Kingdom of the Ganna. He took a few grains and put them in his mouth and chewed them. Once more he put a few grains in his mouth. Then he put a whole handful in his mouth and swallowed. He couldn't stop. He ate and ate. He forgot that this was the corn with which he had to plant his fields. When he arrived in Tendella he went to his bed to sleep, and when he arose the next morning he ate again. He ate so much of the corn that he became sick. He went to his bed again and cried out in pain, because his stomach had forgotten what to do with food. And before long Kaddo died.

Kaddo's grandchildren and great-grandchildren in the Kingdom of Seno are poor to this day. And to the rich men of the country the common people sometimes say:

"Don't build a wall of flour around your house."

"I have a mind to ride over the cliff with you."

The Prince and the Goose Girl

Elinor Mordaunt

Once there was a great prince who was so great a fighter that no one dared to deny him anything that he asked, and people would give up their houses and lands, their children, and even their own freedom rather than offend him. Everything the people had was his at the asking, they feared him so, and would all tremble and shake when he came thundering past on his war horse, whose hoofs struck great pieces of their fields from the earth as he passed, and whose breath was fire. And they feared his sword, which was so sharp that it wounded the wind as it cut through it, and his battle-ax that could cut the world in half—or so they said—and his frown that was like a cloud, and his voice that was like thunder—or so they said.

Only Erith, the goose girl, feared him not at all.

"He is only a man," she would say. "What you tell of his sword and his battle-ax and his great frown is all a child's tale. He is just a man. He eats and sleeps like other men; if you wounded him, he would bleed. Someday he will love a woman and be her slave for a while just as any other man is. I wouldn't give that for the great bully!" she added, and snapped her little fingers.

"Hee, hee, Erith, that's all very well," the folk would say. "Wait till you meet him thundering over the common. You will fly as quick as any of your geese, we wager."

"I wouldn't move. It's a man's place to make room for a lady, not a lady's place to make room for a man.

I wouldn't move, I tell you." And Erith stamped her little foot. It did not seem to impress the village people much, perhaps because it was bare and made no noise on the soft, dusty road, and one needs to make plenty of noise in this world if one is to be noticed.

"A lady! A lady!" they shrieked. "A lord to make place for a lady! Listen to her. My Lady Goosey Gander! A fine lady indeed, with bare feet and no hat."

"There's lots that have shoes that are not ladies," said Erith. "Shoes won't make one, nor bare feet mar one. I'm a better lady than any of you, though, for I'd not run away for anyone, even that ugly old prince. Bah! He's not noble or good or brave; he's just ugly—an ugly great bully!"

"Wait a bit, Lady Goosey Gander, wait a bit. If ever you see him, you will forget all your fine tales. Why, he's as tall as the church."

"And as strong as the sea."

"Why, his hands are like oak trees."

"And he cares no more than death who he attacks."

"Neither do I care," said Erith, setting back her shoulders and tossing her chin. "All men are babies, anyhow!"

The village gasped. That she should dare! She, a chit of a goose girl, to talk of the terror of the whole countryside like that. "All men are babies!" Well, well!

"It's a good thing that you are only what you are, my girl," growled the blacksmith. "For if you were of any account and the prince heard what you said, I would not give a farthing for your life."

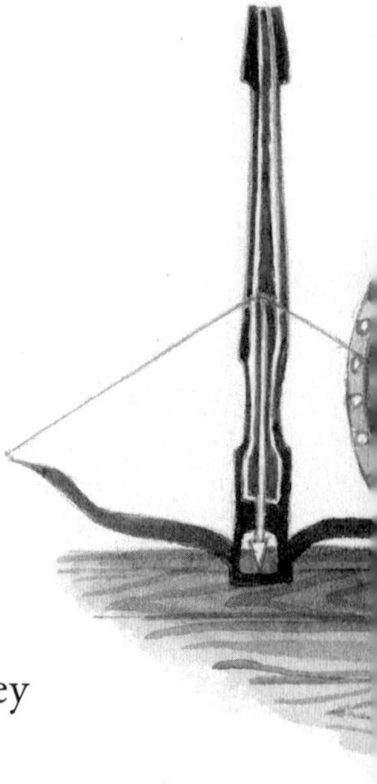

"Hee, hee, Lady Goosey Gander," hooted the children from that day as they passed her on the way to school, tending her geese up on the common; but she only laughed at them, for she was really and truly brave, you know, and really truly brave people do not trouble much about trifles.

One day one of the prince's men heard the children and asked Erith what they meant.

"They call me Lady Goosey Gander because I said I was as good a lady as the prince is a gentleman, and better, for I know enough to be civil and kind," answered Erith, quite unconcerned, busy peeling a willow wand with her little bone-handled knife. She wove these willow wands into baskets while she watched her geese, and sold them in the neighboring market town, for she was poor and had her old mother to keep. She did not stop her work as she spoke; it was more important to her than all the gentlemen or all the princes in the world. She wanted a bag of meal, and she wanted shoes before the winter began. That was her business; other people might attend to their own.

The gentleman was amused. He told his fellows at supper that night and there was much laughter over the goose girl's words. A page waiting at table told his fellows. And then the prince's own man told him as he helped him off with his armor that night.

The prince laughed a great, big, bellowing laugh, but the red swayed up into his face angrily all the same.

"Where does this chit live?" he demanded.

The manservant shrugged his shoulders. "No one knows where she lives; she is of so little importance she might well live nowhere. But she feeds her geese each day on the common above the cliffs to the east, between here and the sea. A barefooted, common little thing."

"There's one thing uncommon enough about her. She dares to say what she thinks about me, and that's more than any of you do. I hear that she is very ugly, though."

"Most terribly ugly, Your Highness," answered the man.

"And old," said the prince.

"Very old, Your Highness. Quite, quite old."

"And deaf, too."

"As deaf as a post, Your Highness. It's evident she has never heard what all your subjects say about you," agreed the man, for he always did agree—he was too frightened to do anything else.

"It is too evident she *has* heard," said the prince grimly. "And she is not deaf."

"Oh, no, Your Highness."

"And she is young."

"Indeed the merest child, Your Highness."

"And beautiful."

"As beautiful as the day, Your Highness."

"Only a country girl, of course, quite uneducated."

"Quite uneducated, Your Highness, and—"

What else he was going to say remained unsaid, for he was stooping over the prince's foot unbuckling his spurs while he spoke, and the prince lifted his foot—quite easily as it seemed—and with it lifted the man, quite easily, but with such force that he bumped against the ceiling, "plump!" and then came to the floor, "bump!"

There were several other men in the room. However, they did not run to pick him up—they were too frightened of their master. But the prince just put out the toe of his other foot and touched him, and he rolled over and over like a ball and down the stairs, limpitty, limpitty, limp.

Then another came forward to undo the other spur, and he was treated the same.

"Take them both out and bury them!" shouted the prince. "And if they're not dead, bury them all the same!" Then he got up and flung around his chamber. He touched no one, but they all fled like hares.

After that he sat down in his great chair, bellowing for wine, and forbade any to go to bed or to sleep, while he sat there himself all night, railing at his men for cowards and fools, and drinking good red wine.

Next morning, directly it was light, the prince ordered his horse, Sable, to be brought around, mounted it, and rode like the wind to the common by the sea.

"That chit of a goose girl is as good as dead," remarked his manservant as best he could for a broken jaw; indeed, you never saw anything so broken; all his legs and arms seemed nothing but splints and bandages. However, it was a common enough sight in the court of that prince, and no one took much notice.

The prince thundered along on his great black horse and presently came to the common. In the middle of it, he saw a flock of white geese and a patch of faded blue, which was the smock of the goose girl, who was sitting on a bundle of willow rods, busy with her basket making.

The prince did not draw rein. He thundered straight on. He scattered the geese in every direction. He would have galloped right over the girl if his horse had not swerved just as its hoofs were upon her. Then he drew rein.

The girl's hands did not stop from her work, but her great blue eyes were straight upon the prince's fierce black ones.

"The beast is less of a beast than the master," she said, for she knew it was the horse that had refused to tread upon her.

The prince pulled his reins, rode back a little, then spurred forward at Erith; but again the horse swerved and, being held with too tight a hand to turn, reared back.

The girl was right under his great pawing black hoofs. But she laughed.

The horse dropped to earth so close that his chest was against hers, his head held high to escape striking her. The foam dropped from his bit; his eye seemed all fire.

The girl's face looked up like a flower from among the thick blackness of his flowing mane. And she laughed again.

This was more than the prince could stand. He stooped from his saddle. He put his great hand into the leather belt of Erith's smock and swung her up in front of him. There he held her with one hand in its iron glove, shook Sable's rein, and put his spurs to his side.

"I have a mind to ride over the cliff with you," said the prince.

"Ride over," laughed Erith. And she took the willow rod that was still in her hand and smote the horse's neck with it. "Over the cliff, brave horse, and a good riddance of a bad man it will be," said she.

But the horse swerved at the edge of the cliff. And the prince let him swerve. Then they turned and they raced like the wind, far, far.

"Are you afraid?" said the prince.

"Afraid!" laughed the girl. She leaned forward along the neck of the horse, caught one little hand around its ear and cried, "Stop!"

Sable stopped so suddenly that his black mane and long black tail flew out like a cloud in front of him.

The prince swore a great oath and smote him, but he did not move.

Then Erith, not willing to see him hurt, whispered, "Go!" And he went—like the wind.

Far, far and fast he went. The prince was brooding too savagely to heed where they were being carried, so that when at length they came to a swamp, the horse, with one of his mighty strides, was borne far into it and sank to his girths before his rider knew what was happening.

You may picture it. The man and the maid and the horse nearly up to their necks in black mud.

Erith was small and light as a bird. She sprang from the arms which were loosed to pull the reins; she caught at a tuft of grass here, at a shrub there, and in a moment was on dry ground, though black to the knees with mire.

But the prince was a tall, great man. He was all in his armor, very heavy, and he could not move except downward; but he flung himself from his horse.

"That's not so bad of him," thought Erith. "He cares to save it, for he himself would have a double chance on its back."

The fierce black eyes of the man and the laughing blue eyes of the goose girl met across the strip of swamp. His were as hard as steel, for he did not mean to beg his life from any such chit.

Erith moved away a little. "She is going to leave me," he thought, and grieved, for he did not wish to die.

The girl had disappeared among a group of trees, but in a moment she came back, dragging after her a large,

thick bough. Then she picked her way cautiously, as near as possible to the edge of the swamp. A little sturdy tree was growing there. Erith undid her leather belt, pressed her back firmly against the tree, and strapped the belt around both it and herself. Then she stretched forward with the bough in both hands.

"Pull," she cried. And the prince pulled.

The little tree creaked and strained. The goose girl's face grew crimson. It seemed as if her arms must be pulled from her body; but she held on, and at last the prince crawled out.

Erith had only been muddied a little above her smock, but the prince was mud up to his armpits, and his face, too, was smeared where he had pushed his helmet back from his forehead with muddy hands. He said no word of thanks to the girl, for he felt that he looked a poor thing, and it made him angry.

"I would I had left you there," said the goose girl. "A thankless boor! You were not worth saving."

The prince said no word, but began to pull out his horse. Even then the maid had to help him, for it was very heavy and deeply sunk.

Once the horse was free, the maid moved over to a pool which lay at the edge of the swamp and began to bathe her feet and legs and wash the mud from the hem of her smock.

The prince got on his horse, with a great deal of clatter and grumbling, but she did not turn. They were many, many miles from home, the country was strange and wild, but there she sat, quite untroubled, paddling her feet in the water.

The prince put his spurs to his horse and galloped away. But the beast would not go freely, spur it as he would. And soon he gave in, let it turn, and so back to the goose girl.

She had dried her feet on the grass by now and was standing plaiting her long hair, eyeing herself in the pool and singing softly.

The prince drew rein close to her and stuck out one foot. "You may come up," he said.

"An' may it please you," corrected the goose girl very quickly, with her blue eyes full upon him.

"May it please you," repeated the prince with a wry smile at himself; and the maid put her foot on his and jumped lightly to the saddle before him.

Sable needed no spur then, but sprang into a light gallop.

"All this is mine," said the prince boastfully, waving his arm as they went.

"I would it belonged to a better man," answered the goose girl. "And sit quietly or I will have no comfort riding with you."

"And you belong to me also," said the prince savagely.

"Not I. I belong to myself, and that is more than you do."

"What do you mean by that?"

"No man belongs to himself who is the slave to evil temper and pride," answered Erith gravely and gently.

After a long ride they came to the common again. On the edge of it was a tiny cottage.

"Stop here," said the goose girl, "and I will get down."

But the prince clapped his spurs to his horse's side and they were off like the wind. Moreover, he held the goose girl's hands so tightly that she could not touch Sable's ear or lean forward and speak to him. And so they galloped on till they clattered over the drawbridge into the courtyard of the castle.

A curious couple they looked. The prince all caked with mud, the goose girl with her wet smock clinging around her bare ankles and her long yellow hair loose, hanging below her knees.

The prince did not get off his horse, but sat like a statue while all the lords and ladies, the captains and the men-at-arms, the pages and the servingmen—even down to the scullery boy—thronged on the terrace and steps and at every window to look.

There was a long silence. Then one lady, who thought she was pretty enough to do as she liked, tittered loudly.

"The Lady Goosey Gander," she said. "The Lady Goosey Gander."

The prince's brow grew like a thundercloud. He flung his reins to one of the waiting grooms and alighted, then gave his hand to Erith, who leaped down as lightly as a bird. Still holding her hand, he turned to his people.

"You are always wishing me to choose a wife," he thundered. "Well, I have chosen one, and here she is. You can call the parson to bring his book and get the wedding feast ready, for I will be married in an hour's time."

With that he pulled off his helmet and flung around to kiss the goose girl, but—

"Shame on you," she cried, "to think to marry a maid before you've asked her! You can marry the cat, for all I care." And with that she caught him a great blow across the face and flung free.

Such a slap, such an echoing, sounding slap. The people of the court did not wait to see what would happen, for they knew what the prince was like in one of his rages all too well, and fled into the palace like rabbits to their burrows—not even a face at the window was left. Only the goose girl did not run, but stood and laughed at the prince's reddened face.

He caught at her wrist, yet not roughly. "You *will* marry me!"

"Perhaps someday when you learn to speak civilly," she replied. And, feeling her wrist free, she marched off over the drawbridge and over the meadow across the

common and so home. She had her own business to attend to.

Some of the prince's people came creeping back. "Shall we go after her, Your Highness?" they asked, thinking to get into his favor again; but he drove them from him with the flat of his great sword and with oaths and shouting, then flung off to his own chamber and sat there drinking red wine till the night was near over; and none of his court as much as dared to go to bed till he slept.

Next morning he was off again at dawn on his black horse across the common. There sat Erith among her geese, weaving baskets. The very horse neighed with joy at the sight of her sitting there in the sunshine, but the prince only scowled.

"Will you marry me?" said he.

"No," said she, "and that's flat—not till you learn manners, at least."

Then he got off his horse and took out his sword and killed all her geese.

"You will have to marry me now or starve, for you have lost all your means of getting a living."

But the girl only laughed and took the dead geese and began plucking them, moving over to the side that the wind blew toward the prince, so that the feathers flew and stuck all over his armor in every chain and crevice and crack; and threw such handfuls of down in his face that when he went to seize her he was powerless.

Next day Erith, having trussed the plucked geese, took them to the market and sold them for a gold piece.

As she came home singing, she met an army of men bearing osier rods. "What have the osiers done that they should all be cut in one day?" she asked.

"The prince sent us to cut them, Lady Goosey Gander," they answered, jeering. "There is not one left at the brook's edge now, and your basket making is spoiled."

But the goose girl only laughed and turned back to the town and bought wool with her gold piece.

Next day as she sat before the fire in her cottage spinning the wool into yarn to sell at the market, the prince came striding in at the little door, bent half double, for it was so low and he so tall with his helmet on his head.

"It is only old women who remain with covered heads in the house," said the goose girl. "Good morning, old dame."

The prince took off his helmet. Somehow her ways pleased him, for he was sick of soft speaking.

"Will you marry me?" said he.

"When you kneel to ask me," said she. "Not before."

Then in a rage he took all her yarn, flung it into the fire, and was out of the house and away, thundering on his great black horse. But the goose girl only laughed.

Then she took a pair of scissors and cut off her long hair, yellow as honey in the comb, and fine as silk. This she spun and wove into a scarf, the rarest scarf ever seen.

On the third day, having finished her work, she was up at dawn and walked off to the court of a king, many miles distant. There she sought the queen and sold her the scarf for twenty pieces of gold.

"But why did you cut off your beautiful hair?" asked the queen.

"It was just forever in the way," replied the goose girl. She told no tales. To begin with, she did not like them, and to end with she *did* like the prince—perhaps because he was as fearless and obstinate as she herself.

Passing through the town, she bought a bag of meal and porridge. "The bag will do to cover my bare poll when it rains," she said to the merchant, and laughed. The gold jangled in the pocket of her petticoat and she felt as gay as a cricket.

On her way back she met the prince, who pulled up his horse and scowled at her, that she might not see the love in his eyes. Her head was all over little golden curls that shone in the sunlight.

"What have you done with your hair?" he asked.

"What have you done with the osiers and the feathers?" she asked in return, and laughed.

"Are you starving yet?"

"Far from it. I am richer than I ever was," and she shook her pocket till all the gold danced, for she feared nothing. But it was a foolish thing to do, for in a moment he had whipped out his sword and cut the pocket clean from the petticoat.

"Now will you marry me?" he asked, and held the pocket high and rattled the gold.

"Not I," she said, "if you are so poor that you'd have to live on your wife's earnings." And went her way singing.

The prince was ashamed of himself. He had never felt like it before, and it was very uncomfortable; it made him feel all tired and hot. It was all the goose girl's fault, of course, and he was very angry. But still he wished he had not stolen her money, and the thought of her little shorn head with its dancing curls made him feel for the first time in his life that he had a heart, and that it hurt.

So wrapped in his shame was the prince and sitting on his horse so loosely, and so heedless of everything that some robbers coming along the road took courage at the sight of him, for he did not look at all terrible as he usually did, and the gold rattled pleasantly. They had passed him many times before and kept their distance; but now they were emboldened to fall upon him, and so sudden was the attack that he was cast from his horse, the gold was gone, and he bound and gagged before he had thought to resist. Such a poor thing can shame make of any one of us.

Before they had finished, Sable had galloped away. "Shall we ride after him?" asked one of the robbers.

"No, no," answered the others. "He is too well known and we should surely be caught." So they mounted their horses and went off, leaving the prince bound and more ashamed of himself than ever. But Sable had galloped straight to the goose girl's cottage and struck at the door with his hoof.

When Erith opened the door, she was amazed to see the horse without his master. He muzzled his soft nose over her neck and hand, then trotted a little distance, then neighed as if to call her and returned. This he did several times.

"There must be something wrong," thought the girl; and she put her foot in the stirrup and leaped to the saddle. "Go like the wind," she whispered, leaning along his neck with one little hand around his ear. And like the wind he went.

Now, the robbers had not much rope to spare, so they had bound the prince kneeling with his arms pulled back and tied to his ankles behind him. And mighty uncomfortable it was. Besides, they had stuck one of their own foul handkerchiefs in his mouth and tied another across and around it. "Anyone who finds me will make a fine mock of me," thought the prince. And he seemed to burn with rage and shame.

But when the goose girl drew up beside him, *she* did not laugh, rather gave a little moan of pity, for the robbers had struck him wantonly over the head and the blood which he could not reach to stanch ran down over his face and eyes.

In a moment she was to the ground, had whipped out the little knife which she still carried in her belt, and cut the bandage and drew the gag from his mouth. She was turning to the ropes around the wrists and ankles then, when—"Stop!" said the prince.

Then, "Will you marry me, Erith?"

"It's a queer time to be asking that," replied the goose girl.

"You charged me to ask on my knees," answered the prince dryly, "and I am here. Will you marry me now?"

"An' it please you," corrected she, with calm blue eyes.

"An' it please you, dear heart," said he, almost meekly. "And we will not be living on your money, for it is all gone."

"Well, I don't mind if I do," answered the goose girl, and cut the ropes.

So they were trothed and kissed one another. And the prince put her on the front of his own horse and rode with her to the court, where he told the queen all that had happened and charged her, by her friendship, to get all manner of beautiful raiment and jewels ready and command a great feast that he might marry the goose girl one week from that day, she consenting.

It was the sunniest day ever known in all the world, and the gayest wedding and the fairest bride. And the feasting and dancing lasted for seven days, and there was none in the whole country who went hungry or without a share of the pleasures.

On the seventh day the prince took his bride back to his own kingdom. They would have no coach, but rode Sable over the hills and pastures and across the common where the geese had once fed, and over the drawbridge and home.

The new princess had little golden slippers on her feet now, and a robe of rose silk all embroidered with pearls, and a cloak of ermine. But her head was bare, with no crown save that of short golden curls.

Theme Introduction

Compassion

In this section of the book, you will read about characters who are compassionate, and characters who struggle with compassion. Thinking about these stories, and about your own experiences, will give you new ideas about what it means to be compassionate.

Important Questions to Think About

Before starting this section, think about your experiences with compassion:

- Can you think of a time when someone showed you compassion?
- What makes you feel compassion toward others?

Once you have thought about your own experiences with compassion, think about this **theme question** and write down your answers or share them aloud:

What makes a person compassionate?

After reading each story in this section, ask yourself the theme question again. You may have some new ideas you want to add.

"Louie! Louis! Where are you?"

A Bad Road for Cats

Cynthia Rylant

Louie! Louis! Where are you?"

The woman called it out again and again as she walked along Route 6. A bad road for cats. She prayed he hadn't wandered this far. But it had been nearly two weeks, and still Louis hadn't come home.

She stopped at a Shell station, striding up to the young man at the register. Her eyes snapped black and fiery as she spit the question at him:

"Have you seen a *cat*?" The word *cat* came out hard as a rock.

The young man straightened up.

"No, ma'am. No cats around here. Somebody dropped a mutt off a couple nights ago, but a Mack truck got it yesterday about noon. Dog didn't have a chance."

The woman's eyes pinched his.

"I lost my cat. Orange and white. If you see him, you be more careful of him than that dog. This is a bad road for cats."

She marched toward the door.

"I'll be back," she said, like a threat, and the young man straightened up again as she went out.

"Louie! Louis! Where are you?"

She was a very tall woman, and skinny. Her black hair was long and shiny, like an Indian's. She might have been a Cherokee making her way alongside a river, alert and watchful. Tracking.

But Route 6 was no river. It was a truckers' road, lined with gas stations, motels, dairy bars, diners. A nasty road, smelling of diesel and rubber.

The woman's name was Magda. And she was of French blood, not Indian. Magda was not old, but she carried herself as a very old and strong person might, with no fear of death and with a clear sense of her right to the earth and a disdain for the ugliness of belching machines and concrete.

Magda lived in a small house about two miles off Route 6. There she worked at a loom, weaving wool gathered from the sheep she owned. Magda's husband was dead, and she had no children. Only a cat named Louis.

Dunh. Dunh. Duuunnh.

Magda's heart pounded as a tank truck roared by. *Duuunnh.* The horn hurt her ears, making her feel sick inside, stealing some of her strength.

Four years before, Magda had found Louis at one of the gas stations on Route 6. She had been on her way home from her weekly trip to the grocery and had pulled in for a fill-up. As she'd stood inside the station in front of the cigarette machine, dropping in quarters, she'd felt warm fur against her leg and had given a start. Looking down, she'd seen an orange and white kitten. It had purred and meowed and pushed its nose into Magda's shoes. Smiling, Magda had picked the kitten up. Then she had seen the horror.

Half of the kitten's tail was gone. What remained was bloody and scabbed, and the stump stuck straight out.

Magda had carried the animal to one of the station attendants.

"Whose kitten is this?" Her eyes drilled in the question.

The attendant had shrugged his shoulders.

"Nobody's. Just a drop-off."

Magda had moved closer to him.

"What happened to its *tail*?" she asked, the words slow and clear.

"Got caught in the door. Stupid cat was under everybody's feet—no wonder half its tail got whacked."

Magda could not believe such a thing.

"And you offer it no help?" she had asked.

"Not my cat," he answered.

Magda's face had blazed as she'd turned and stalked out the door with the kitten.

A veterinarian mended what was left of the kitten's tail. And Magda named it Louis for her grandfather.

"Louie! Louis! Where are you?"

Dunh. Duuunnh. Another horn at her back. Magda wondered about her decision to walk Route 6 rather than drive it. She had thought that on foot she might find Louis more easily—in a ditch, under some bushes, up a tree. They were even, she and Louis, if she were on foot, too. But the trucks were making her misery worse.

Magda saw a dairy bar up ahead. She thought she would stop and rest. She would have some coffee and a slice of quiet away from the road.

She walked across the wide gravel lot to the tiny walk-up window. Pictures of strawberry sundaes, spongy shakes, cones with curly peaks were plastered all over the building, drawing business from the road with big red words like *CHILLY.*

Magda barely glanced at the young girl working inside. All teenage girls looked alike to her.

"Coffee," she ordered.

"Black?"

"Yes."

Magda moved to one side and leaned against the building. The trucks were rolling out on the highway, but far enough away to give her time to regain her strength. No horns, no smoke, no dirt. A little peace.

She drank her coffee and thought about Louis when he was a kitten. Once, he had leaped from her attic window and she had found him, stunned and shivering, on the hard gravel below. The veterinarian said Louis had broken a leg and was lucky to be alive. The kitten had stomped around in a cast for a few weeks. Magda drew funny faces on it to cheer him up.

Louis loved white cheese, tall grass, and the skeins of wool Magda left lying around her loom.

That's what she would miss most, she thought, if Louis never came back: an orange and white cat making the yarn fly under her loom.

Magda finished her coffee, then turned to throw the empty cup in the trash can. As she did, a little sign in the bottom corner of the window caught her eye. The words were surrounded by dirty smudges:

Magda caught her breath. She moved up to the window and this time looked squarely into the face of the girl.

"Are you selling a *cat*?" she said quietly, but hard on *cat*.

"Not me. This boy," the girl answered, brushing her stringy hair back from her face.

"Where is he?" Magda asked.

"That yellow house right off the road up there."

Magda headed across the lot.

She had to knock only once. The door opened and standing there was a boy about fifteen.

"I saw your sign," Magda said. "I am interested in your cat."

The boy did not answer. He looked at Magda's face with his wide blue eyes, and he grinned, showing a mouth of rotten and missing teeth.

Magda felt a chill move over her.

"The cat," she repeated. "You have one to sell? Is it orange and white?"

The boy stopped grinning. Without a word, he slammed the door in Magda's face.

She was stunned. A strong woman like her, to be so stunned by a boy. It shamed her. But again she knocked on the door—and very hard this time.

No answer.

What kind of boy is this? Magda asked herself. A strange one. And she feared he had Louis.

She had just raised her hand to knock a third time when the door opened. There the boy stood with Louis in his arms.

Again, Magda was stunned. Her cat was covered with oil and dirt. He was thin, and his head hung weakly. When he saw Magda, he seemed to use his last bit of strength to let go a pleading cry.

The boy no longer was grinning. He held Louis close against him, forcefully stroking the cat's ears again and again and again. The boy's eyes were full of tears, his mouth twisted into sad protest.

Magda wanted to leap for Louis, steal him, and run for home. But she knew better. This was an unusual boy. She must be careful.

Magda put her hand into her pocket and pulled out a dollar bill.

"*Enough?*" she asked, holding it up.

The boy clutched the cat harder, his mouth puckering fiercely.

Magda pulled out two more dollar bills. She held the money up, the question in her eyes.

The boy relaxed his hold on Louis. He tilted his head to one side, as if considering Magda's offer.

Then, in desperation, Magda pulled out a twenty-dollar bill.

"*Enough?*" she almost screamed.

The boy's head jerked upright, then he grabbed all the bills with one hand and shoved Louis at Magda with the other.

Magda cradled Louis in her arms, rubbing her cheek across his head. Before walking away, she looked once more at the boy. He stood stiffly with the money clenched in his hand, tears running from his eyes and dripping off his face like rainwater.

Magda took Louis home. She washed him and healed him. And for many days she was in a rage at the strange boy who had sold her her own cat, nearly dead.

When Louis was healthy, though, and his old fat self, playing games among the yarn beneath her loom, her rage grew smaller and smaller until finally she could forgive the strange boy.

She came to feel sympathy for him, remembering his tears. And she wove some orange and white wool into a pattern, stuffed it with cotton, sewed two green button eyes and a small pink mouth onto it, then attached a matching stub of a tail.

She put the gift in a paper bag, and, on her way to the grocery one day, she dropped the bag in front of the boy's yellow house.

"You can come home to tea with me."

LENNY'S RED-LETTER DAY

Bernard Ashley

Lenny Fraser is a boy in my class. Well, he's a boy in my class when he comes. But to tell the truth, he doesn't come very often. He stays away from school for a week at a time, and I'll tell you where he is. He's at the shops, stealing things sometimes, but mainly just opening the doors for people. He does it to keep himself warm. I've seen him in our shop. When he opens the door for someone, he stands around inside till he gets sent out. Of course, it's quite warm enough in school, but he hates coming. He's always got long, tangled hair, not very clean, and his clothes are too big or too small, and they call him "Fleabag." He sits at a desk without a partner, and no one wants to hold his hand in games. All right, they're not to blame; but he isn't, either. His mother never gets up in the morning, and his house is dirty. It's a house that everybody runs past very quickly.

But Lenny makes me laugh a lot. In the playground, he's always saying funny things out of the corner of his mouth. He doesn't smile when he does it. He says these funny things as if he's complaining. For example, when Mr. Cox the deputy head came to school in his new car, Lenny came too, that day; but he didn't join in all the admiration. He looked at the little car and said to me, "Anyone missing a skateboard?"

He misses all the really good things, though—the School Journeys and the outing. And it was a big shame about his birthday.

It happens like this with birthdays in our class. Miss Blake lets everyone bring their cards and perhaps a small present to show the others. Then everyone sings "Happy Birthday" and we give them bumps in the playground. If people can't bring a present, they tell everyone what they've got instead. I happen to know some people make up the things that they've got just to be up with the others, but Miss Blake says it's good to share our Red-Letter Days.

I didn't know about these Red-Letter Days before. I thought they were something special in the post, like my dad handles in his Post Office in the shop. But Miss Blake told us they are red printed words in the prayer books, meaning special days.

Well, what I'm telling you is that Lenny came to school on his birthday this year. Of course, he didn't tell us it was his birthday, and, as it all worked out, it would have been better if Miss Blake hadn't noticed it in the register. But, "How nice!" she said. "Lenny's here on his birthday, and we can share it with him."

It wasn't very nice for Lenny. He didn't have any cards to show the class, and he couldn't think of a birthday present to tell us about. He couldn't even think of anything funny to say out of the corner of his mouth. He just had to stand there looking foolish until Miss Blake started the singing of "Happy Birthday"—and then half the people didn't bother to sing it. I felt very sorry for him, I can tell you. But that wasn't the worst. The worst happened in the playground. I went to take his head end for bumps, and no one would come and take his feet. They all walked away. I had to finish up just patting him on the head with my hands, and before I knew what was coming out I was telling him, "You can come home to tea with me, for your birthday." And he said, yes, he would come.

My father works very hard in the Post Office, in a corner of our shop; and my mother stands at the door all day, where people pay for their groceries. When I get home from school, I carry cardboard boxes out to the yard and jump on them, or my big sister Nalini shows me which shelves to fill and I fill them with jam or chapatis—or birthday cards. On this day, though, I thought I'd use my key and go in through the side door and take Lenny straight upstairs—then hurry down again and tell my mum and dad that I'd got a friend in for an hour. I thought, I can get a birthday card and some cake and ice cream from the shop, and Lenny can go home before they come upstairs. I wanted him to do that before my dad saw who it was, because he knows Lenny from his hanging around the shops.

Lenny said some funny things on the way home from school, but you know, I couldn't relax and enjoy them properly. I felt ashamed because I was wishing all the time that I hadn't asked him to come home with me. The bottoms of his trousers dragged along the ground, he had no buttons on his shirt so the sleeves flapped, and his hair must have made it hard for him to see where he was going.

I was in luck because the shop was very busy. My dad had a queue of people to pay out, and my mum had a crowd at the till. I left Lenny in the living room and I went down to get what I wanted from the shop. I found him a birthday card with a badge in it. When I came back, he was sitting in a chair and the television was switched

on. He's a good one at helping himself, I thought. We watched some cartoons and then we played Monopoly, which Lenny had seen on the shelf. We had some crisps and cakes and lemonade while we were playing; but I had only one eye on my Monopoly moves—the other eye was on the clock all the time. I was getting very impatient for the game to finish, because it looked as if Lenny would still be there when they came up from the shop. I did some really bad moves so that I could lose quickly, but it's very difficult to hurry up Monopoly, as you may know.

In the end I did such stupid things—like buying too many houses and selling Park Lane and Mayfair—that he won the game. He must have noticed what I was doing, but he didn't say anything to me. Hurriedly, I gave him his birthday card. He pretended not to take very much notice of it, but he put it in his shirt, and

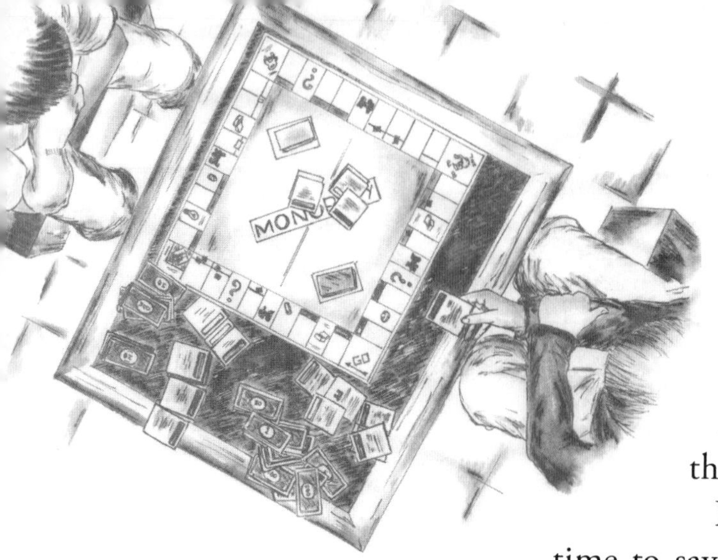

kept feeling it to make sure it was still there. At least, that's what I thought he was making sure about, there inside his shirt.

It was just the right time to say goodbye, and I'm just thinking he can go without anyone seeing him, when my sister came in. She had run up from the shop for something or other, and she put her head inside the room. At some other time, I would have laughed out loud at her stupid face. When she saw Lenny, she looked as if she'd opened the door and seen something really unpleasant. I could gladly have given her a good kick. She shut the door a lot quicker than she opened it, and I felt really bad about it.

"Nice to meet you," Lenny joked, but his face said he wanted to go, too, and I wasn't going to be the one to stop him.

I let him out, and I heaved a big sigh. I felt good about being kind to him, the way you do when you've done a sponsored swim, and I'd done it without my mum and dad frowning at me about who I brought home. Only Nalini had seen him, and everyone knows she can make things seem worse than they are. I washed the glasses, and I can remember singing while I stood at the sink. I was feeling very pleased with myself.

My good feeling lasted about fifteen minutes; just long enough to be wearing off slightly. Then Nalini came in again and destroyed it altogether.

"Prakash, have you seen that envelope that was on the television top?" she asked. "I put it on here when I came in from school."

"No," I said. It was very soon to be getting worried, but things inside me were turning over like clothes in a washing machine. I knew already where all this was going to end up. "What was in it?" My voice sounded to me as if it was coming from a great distance.

She was looking everywhere in the room, but she kept coming back to the television top as if the envelope would mysteriously appear there. She stood there now, staring at me. "*What was in it?* What was in it was only a Postal Order for five pounds! Money for my school trip!"

"What does it look like?" I asked, but I think we both knew that I was only stalling. We both knew where it had gone.

"It's a white piece of paper in a brown envelope. It says 'Postal Order' on it, in red."

My washing machine inside nearly went into a fast spin when I heard that. It was certainly Lenny's Red-Letter Day! But how could he be so ungrateful, I thought, when I was the only one to be kind to him? I clenched my fist while I pretended to look around. I wanted to punch him hard on the nose.

Then Nalini said what was in both our minds. "It's that dirty kid who's got it. I'm going down to tell Dad. I don't know what makes you so stupid."

Right at that moment I didn't know what made me so stupid, either, as to leave him up there on his own. I should have known. Didn't Miss Banks once say something about leopards never changing their spots?

When the shop closed, there was an awful business in the room. My dad was shouting-angry at me, and my mum couldn't think of anything good to say.

"You know where this boy lives," my dad said. "Tell me now, while I telephone the police. There's only one way of dealing with this sort of thing. If I go up there, I shall only get a mouthful of abuse. As if it isn't bad enough for you to see me losing things out of the shop, you have to bring untrustworthy people upstairs!"

My mum saw how unhappy I was, and she tried to make things better. "Can't you cancel the Postal Order?" she asked him.

"Of course not. Even if he hasn't had the time to cash it somewhere else by now, how long do you think the Post Office would let me be Sub-Postmaster if I did that sort of thing?"

I was feeling very bad for all of us, but the thought of the police calling at Lenny's house was making me feel worse.

"I'll get it back," I said. "I'll go to his house. It's only along the road from the school. And if I don't get it back, I can get the exact number of where he lives. *Then* you can telephone the police." I had never spoken to my dad like that before, but I was feeling all shaky inside, and all the world seemed a different place to me that evening. I didn't give anybody a chance to argue with me. I ran straight out of the room and down to the street.

My secret hopes of seeing Lenny before I got to his house didn't come to anything. All too quickly I was there, pushing back his broken gate and walking up the cracked path to his front door. There wasn't a door knocker. I flapped the letter box, and I started to think my dad was right. The police would have been better doing this than me.

I had never seen his mother before, only heard about her from other kids who lived near. When she opened the door, I could see she was a small lady with a tight mouth and eyes that said, "Who are you?" and "Go away from here!" at the same time.

She opened the door only a little bit, ready to slam it on me. I had to be quick.

"Is Lenny in, please?" I asked her.

She said, "What's it to you?"

"He's a friend of mine," I told her. "Can I see him, please?"

She made a face as if she had something nasty in her mouth. "LENNY!" she shouted. "COME HERE!"

Lenny came slinking down the passage, like one of those scared animals in a circus. He kept his eyes on her hands, once he'd seen who it was at the door. There weren't any funny remarks coming from him.

She jerked her head at me. "How many times have I told you not to bring kids to the house?" she shouted at him. She made it sound as if she was accusing him of a bad crime.

Lenny had nothing to say. She was hanging over him like a vulture about to fix its talons into a rabbit. It looked so out of place that it didn't seem real. Then it came to me that it could be play-acting—the two of them. He had given her the five pounds, and she was putting this on to get rid of me quickly.

But suddenly she slammed the door so hard in my face I could see how the glass in it came to be broken.

"Well, I don't want kids coming to my door!" she shouted at him on the other side. "Breaking the gate, breaking the windows, wearing out the path. How can I keep this place nice when I'm forever dragging to the door?"

She hit him then, I know she did. There was no play-acting about the bang as a foot hit the door, and Lenny yelling out loud as if a desk lid had come down on his head. But I didn't stop to hear any more. I'd heard enough to turn my stomach sick. Poor Lenny—I'd been worried about my mum and dad seeing him—and look what happened when his mother saw me! She had to be mad, that woman. And Lenny had to live with her! I didn't feel like crying, although my eyes had a hot rawness in them. More than anything, I just wanted to be back at home with my own family and the door shut tight.

Seeing my dad's car turn the corner was as if my dearest wish had been granted. He was going slowly, searching for me, with Nalini sitting up in front with big eyes. I waved, and ran to them. I got in the back and I drew in my breath to tell them to go straight home. It was worth fifty pounds not to have them knocking at Lenny's house, never mind five. But they were too busy trying to speak to me.

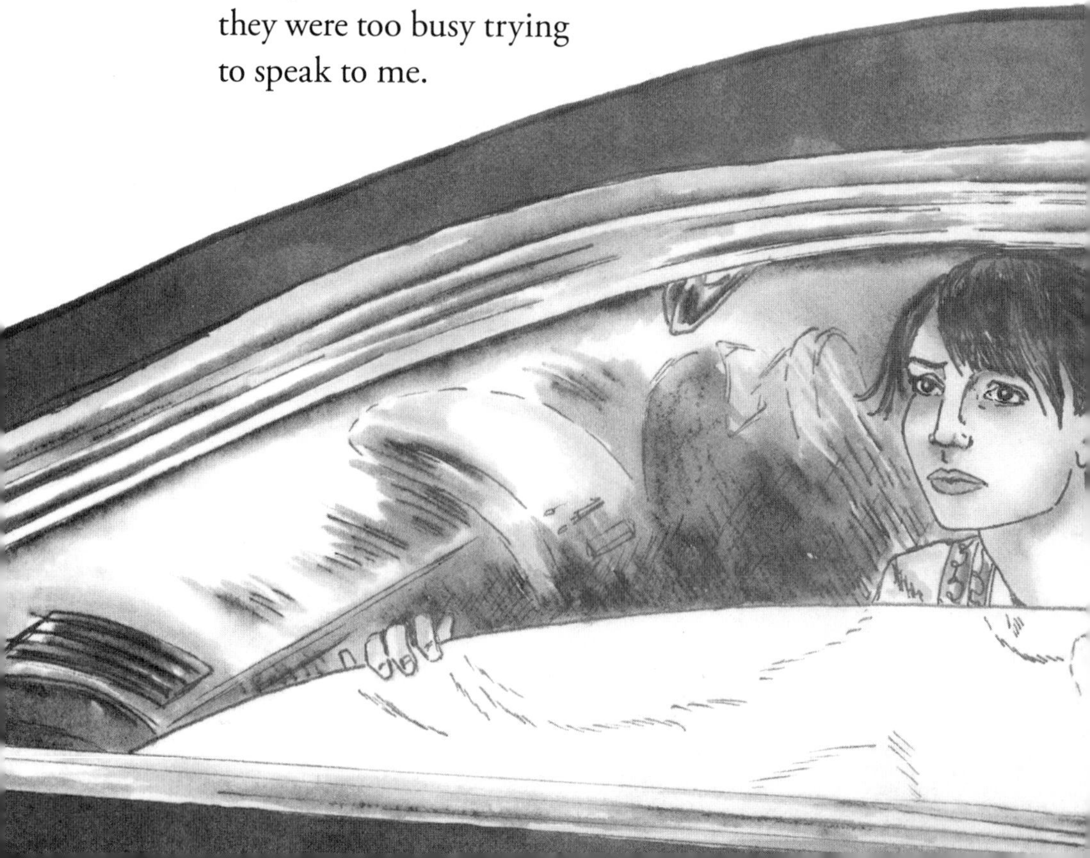

"Have you been to the house? Did you say anything?"

"Yes, I've been to the house, but—"

"Did you accuse him?"

"No. I didn't have a chance—"

They both sat back in their seats, as if the car would drive itself home.

"Well, we must be grateful for that."

"We found the Postal Order."

I could hardly believe what my ears were hearing. *They had found the Postal Order.* Lenny hadn't taken it, after all!

"It wasn't in its envelope," Nalini was saying. "He must have taken it out of that when he was tempted by it. But we can't accuse him of screwing up an envelope and hiding it in his pocket."

"No, no," I was saying, urging her to get on with things and tell me. "So where was it?"

"In with the Monopoly money. He couldn't put it back on the television, so he must have kept it in his pile of Monopoly money, and put it back in the box."

"Oh."

"Mum found it. In all the commotion after you went out she knocked the box off the chair, and when she picked the bits up, there was the Postal Order."

"It's certainly a good job you said nothing about it," my dad said. "And a good job I didn't telephone the police. We should have looked very small."

All I could think was how small I had just felt, standing at Lenny's slammed door and hearing what his mother had said to him. And what about him getting beaten for having a friend call at his house?

My dad tried to be cheerful. "Anyway, who won?" he asked.

"Lenny won the Monopoly, " I said.

In bed that night, I lay awake a long time, thinking about it all. Lenny had taken some hard punishment from his mother. Some Red-Letter Day it had turned out to be! He would bear some hard thoughts about Prakash Patel.

He didn't come to school for a long time after that. But when he did, my heart sank into my boots. He came straight across the playground, the same flappy sleeves and dragging trouser bottoms, the same long, tangled hair—and he came straight for me. What would he do? Hit me? Spit in my face?

As he got close, I saw what was on his shirt, pinned there like a medal. It was his birthday badge.

"It's a good game, that Monopoly," he said out of the corner of his mouth. It was as if he was trying to tell me something.

"Yes," I said. "It's a good game all right."

I hadn't got the guts to tell him that I'd gone straight home that night and thrown it in the dustbin. Dealings with houses didn't appeal to me anymore.

It was near midnight when they entered the mickle woods.

Through the Mickle Woods

Valiska Gregory

At eventide the king sat on a solitary throne. Winter snow drummed its fingers on the windows, and icicles hung like daggers from the roof.

"I am weary," he said. He drew his cloak around him like a crow folding black wings and closed his eyes.

The boy Michael stood before him holding a carved box. "It is a gift," he said. There were bells on the boy's hat, but since the death of the queen, he too wore black.

The king sighed. "It might help pass the time," he said. And so it was the great king opened the box.

Inside, there was an opal ring, flecked blue as the boy's eyes, and a letter sealed with wax. The king said not a word.

"It's the queen's ring," explained Michael. "She asked me to give it to you when she was gone."

The king's hands trembled as he opened the letter. He read the queen's words written plain as footsteps in the snow:

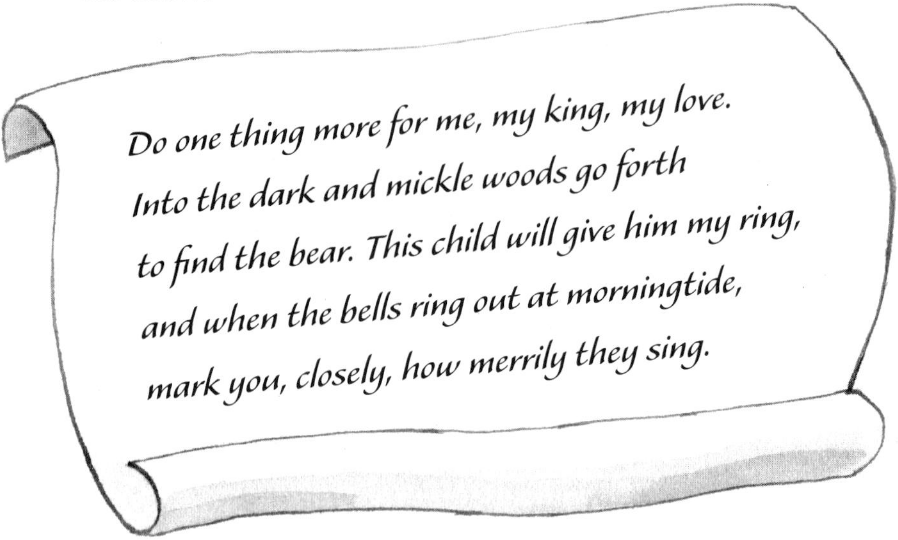
Do one thing more for me, my king, my love.
Into the dark and mickle woods go forth
to find the bear. This child will give him my ring,
and when the bells ring out at morningtide,
mark you, closely, how merrily they sing.

The king stared at the letter a long time before speaking. "I will not make this journey," he said. "It is not fitting for a king in mourning."

"But she said it was important," said Michael. "I promised her."

The king's eyes glinted black. "Then we will go," he said finally, "but only because she wished it."

They walked in silence through the dark. Michael's eyes were bright, and he tried to catch a snowflake with his tongue. "Can you see?" he said. "My breath makes words in the air." He breathed out like a dragon and laughed.

"The way is hard," said the king. "You'd best save your breath."

"But it is so beautiful," said the boy. "The snow looks like sugar in the moonlight." He flapped his arms like a bird. "Watch me. See how my shadow flies?"

The king did not stop. "I have had enough of shadows," he said.

For hours the boy kept pace with the king, but increasingly he lagged behind. He stopped once to watch an owl, and another time he rested on the stump of a tree, but he did not complain.

The king watched as Michael struggled to catch up. "We will try to find a place to rest," he said.

They walked together through the cold until they saw a light, small as a firefly, from a cottage in the distance.

"Come in, come in," said the old woman at the cottage door. She hobbled to the fireside, her back bent like a shepherd's crook.

"Do you not know me?" said the king.

"I know you are a stranger who needs a bit of bread," she said, "and that's enough." She stirred the fire and yellow cinders danced like summer bees.

The king sat, rigid and dark, near the door. "I am used to the cold," he said.

"Suit yourself," said the old woman. She handed Michael a thick slice of buttered bread and plumped a quilt around his knees. "And will you stay the night?" she asked.

"We can rest only a little while," said the king. "We seek the old bear."

The woman wiped her hands on her apron. "They say," she said, "the bear is as fierce as he is wise."

Michael shivered.

"They said," said the woman, "the bear is as old as earth itself."

"Enough," said the king. "We must go."

As they left, the old woman wrapped a scarf around Michael's face. "Take care of this lad," she said to the king. "Keep him warm and safe." She stood in the doorway and watched them, until their distant shapes, like candles in the night, flickered and went out.

It was near midnight when they entered the mickle woods. The moon peeked through the black fingers of the trees, and Michael heard wolves howling in the distance.

"Stay close," said the king sharply. "I would not lose you too."

Michael looked up. "The queen said that to me once," he said. "It was after my mother and father died, and I was crying because I'd gotten lost in the castle."

The king did not respond.

"She told me I didn't have to be scared, because she would always take care of me," said the boy. He shivered in the cold wind. "I miss her," he said.

"I will not talk of this," said the king. "Come quickly now."

They walked together silently, and by midnight they arrived at the cave.

"We must wait here until we are called," said the king. He looked at Michael's questioning face. "My father brought me here," he explained, "to hear the old stories."

Michael moved closer to the king. "The queen used to tell me stories," he whispered, but the king turned his back as if the boy had not spoken.

It was not long before Michael heard the bear's voice. Deep, like the rumbling of mountains, the sound circled round him like a cloak.

"Come," said the bear from within, and slowly they entered the cave.

Michael saw the candles first, hundreds of candles that flickered brown shadows on the walls. And then he saw the bear himself, large and golden as a haystack, seated in a carved oak chair.

"My queen is dead," said the king, motioning the boy forward. "She asked that we bring you her ring."

The bear growled low, like the sighing of the wind. "It has been a long time since you came to me," he said. "Have you a question?"

"Why ask questions when there are no answers?" said the king. He turned as if to go, but the boy tugged on his arm.

"The stories," Michael whispered, "what about the stories?"

"We have done what the queen asked," said the king.

"But could we hear just one?"

"We have no need to stay longer," said the king.

The bear growled again, and this time Michael felt the ground tremble beneath his feet.

"You have more need than you know," said the bear. He drew them nearer to the fire. "Consider this," he said.

In a kingdom long ago there was a man who traveled from the farthest city to the nearest town. And as he went he traded things—a pair of shoes for a piece of gold, a parrot for a bolt of silver cloth—until he was more rich than he had ever dreamed possible. The people thought a man who had so many things must be wise, and no matter where he went they followed him, asking questions.

"Our baby cries," said one. "What should we do?"

"My father went to war. How will we live?" said another.

But though the traveling man could fetch goods from his sack and add up sums, he could not answer their questions.

One day he met an old woman who carried a wooden box. "Inside this box," she said, "are answers to all things."

The traveling man whistled. "I have seen many things," he said, "but I would give all I have to open that box."

"Done," said the old woman.

When the traveling man lifted the lid, he saw to his surprise that the box was filled with coins. Each one was stamped with a curious sentence. "Open the door," said one. "Give him your love," said another. "One hundred and five," said a third.

The traveling man was overjoyed. "I am rich beyond measure," he said. "I have answers to all things."

The old woman smiled. "But what good is an answer," she said, "without the right question?"

The king stared at the fire. "But this traveling man was not a king," he said. "He was not a man whose queen was dead."

"Whether we are born high or low," said the bear, "the same things come to us all."

Michael moved a little closer to the bear. "The queen used to say I asked more questions than there are flowers in the meadow."

The old bear drew him closer still, and Michael felt the warmth of his fur. "One day," said the boy, "I asked the queen why black-eyed Susans have only one eye, and she laughed. I liked it when she laughed."

The king scowled. "Enough of this talk," he said. "I have given you the queen's ring as she asked, and we shall not stay longer."

This time the bear's growl shook the walls of the cave and made the candles flutter like moths. "Consider this," he said.

In a kingdom long ago there was a man who lived alone. In spring he never sowed his seeds for fear there might be drought, and in fall he would not travel lest his ship be blown into the deep. But though he locked his doors inside and out, it did not bring him peace.

One day a bird, small and slight as a pebble, flew to his window. He marveled at her green wings and at the beauty of her song.

"I have heard that wind can uproot a tree from the ground," said the man. "Are you not afraid of wind?"

The bird cocked her head brightly. "Of course," she said.

"And I have heard that fire can sweep a forest in a day," the man said. "Are you not afraid of fire?"

"Yes," she said. Her wings, thin as pages in a book, glinted in the yellow sunlight.

"But if you are afraid," asked the man, "why do you fly? Why do you build your nest?"

The bird cracked a grain of millet in her beak. "There are things I would not miss," she said. "Every day there is morning, ripe as a peach." She trilled a score of grace notes effortlessly. "And fledglings in the spring, of course—small things."

"I do not wish to hear of these," said the man. "What of wind and fire?"

The bird considered thoughtfully. "My song," she said finally, "requires them all." The man watched her fly away, as frail and strong as ashes dancing in the air.

Michael looked up and smiled at the bear. "And was the man always afraid?"

"He made his choice," said the bear, "as must we all."

The king moved closer to the fire. "It is not as easy as the bird suggests," he said.

"No," said the bear, "it is not easy."

Michael pulled his knees up to his chin. "The bird in the story reminded me of the queen. She loved to sing."

The king stared at Michael thoughtfully. When he finally spoke, his voice seemed crumbled, like the embers of the fire. "I cannot remember the sound of her voice," he whispered.

"It was like bells," said the boy. "Listen." He jingled the bells on the hat the queen had made him.

"I'd forgotten that," said the king.

"And her hands," said Michael, "do you remember how she used to make things?"

"She had small hands," said the king. He shuddered and for a moment could not speak. "I do not think I can bear to remember all of it," he said.

The bear growled low, his words bending round them like a lullaby. "Can you bear to remember less?" he asked. "Consider this:"

In a kingdom long ago there was a weaver who spun stories out of thread. One day an owl as white as winter perched in a nearby tree. "I should like my story to be woven out of clouds," said the owl.

"As you wish," said the weaver. The owl brought the woman strings of clouds as round as pearls, but every time she tried to weave them in and out, they would dissolve as quietly as dew upon the grass.

The owl blinked his great eyes. "Perhaps we should add some moonlight," he said, "the kind that shimmers on the water."

"As you wish," said the weaver. But though the owl brought baskets of jeweled moonbeams, worth more than the king's own crown, the story's cloth would not take shape.

"I do not understand," said the owl. "I have chosen beautiful things for the weaving of my story."

"Ah," said the woman. "But sometimes the cloth will pattern itself whether we will or no. You must bring everything, things chosen and things not."

The owl flew over mountains and through valleys. He gathered jade, green as ginkgo leaves, and raspberries, red as blood. He flew past peaceful villages and countries ravaged by war, and when he returned with all the things that he had found, the weaver smiled.

"These will do," she said. She took the things the owl had brought—threads of sunlight fine as silk and cobwebs gray as skulls—and wove them all together into a cloth. And when the owl pulled his story round him, it was so full of woe and gladness, so beautiful and strong, that when he stretched out his new-made wings, people thought he was an angel hovering in a breathless sky.

"So it was," said the bear, "and so it will forever be."

The king sat alone without saying a word. He turned to the boy, his face white as bones. Slowly and deliberately, he reached out his hand. "Do you remember," he said softly, "how she loved all things?"

Michael hesitated. Then, timid and brave as a sparrow, he climbed into the king's lap. "If I was sad," he said, "she would hold me."

"So she did," said the king.

He cradled Michael in his arms, as through the long night they slept, their dreams entwined like holly branches in a wreath. When morning came, they left the mickle woods.

They walked swiftly, stopping to rest only

at the old woman's cottage. Michael laughed as they stomped snow from their feet and knocked on the door.

"We thank you for your kindness last night," said the king. Fluttering about like a gray dove, the old woman made them wait until she'd wrapped a loaf of bread for the journey home. Before they left, the king pressed three gold coins into her hand.

"It is small payment for bread so freely given," he said.

The king walked steadily as Michael ran ahead, then ran back, never seeming to tire.

"Look!" Michael said, and they watched the orange sun deftly escape the tangled web of branches above them.

When they were near enough to see the smoke from their own hearth, Michael stopped. "Listen," he said. "It's the morning bells!"

The king smiled. The snow, crisp and even as parchment, lay before them, and the bells rang out strong and clear. He reached down and took hold of Michael's small hand as if it were a gift of great price.

"Mark you," said the king, "how merrily they ring."

A Guide to Question Types

Below are different types of questions you might ask while reading. Notice that it isn't always important (or even possible) to answer all questions right away. The questions below are about "Kamau's Finish" (pp. 15–25).

Factual questions are about the story and have one correct answer that you can find by looking back at the story.	Why does Kamau fall down during the race? (Answer: He falls down because Kip pushes him.) Why does Baba say he might not be able to come to the race? (Answer: He has an important business meeting.)
Vocabulary questions are about words or phrases in the story. They can be answered with the glossary (pp. 167–184), a dictionary, or *context clues*—parts of the story near the word that give hints about its meaning.	What does "elated" mean? What is "murram dust"? (Practice finding context clues on page 16 to figure out the meaning of this phrase.)
Background questions are often about a story's location, time period, or culture. You can answer them with information from a source like the Internet or an encyclopedia.	What country is Nairobi in? What does maziwa lala taste like?

Speculative questions ask about events or details that are not covered in the story. You must guess at or invent your answers.	Would Kamau have won the race if he didn't fall? Will Baba come to Kamau's next race?
Evaluative questions ask for your personal opinion about something in the story, like whether a character does the right thing. These questions have more than one good answer. Support for these answers comes from your beliefs and experiences as well as the story.	Is Kamau foolish to believe in uganga magic? Was it wrong for Mami to call Kamau selfish for asking Baba to come to the race?
Interpretive questions ask about the deep meaning of the story and are the focus of a Shared Inquiry discussion. They have more than one good answer. Support for these answers comes only from evidence in the story.	Why does Kamau get up and finish the race? Why doesn't Baba say anything when Mami is scolding Kamau?

Shared Inquiry Beyond the Classroom

The skills you have practiced in Junior Great Books will help you in school, but they will also help you in other parts of your life. Through your practice with Shared Inquiry you've learned to:

Ask questions. To learn almost anything, you need to ask questions. If you want to know how to program a computer, play chess, or bake a cake, questions can help you understand what to do and why. The first step to understanding is expressing what you don't understand, and asking questions to find out more helps you learn something *really* well.

Think deeply and search for meaning. By discussing stories, you've learned that you can understand more by going deeper. Lots of things in life are like this, such as movies, art, and the natural world. Spending time looking closely at things and wondering about them helps you understand more about the world around you.

Back up your ideas with evidence. Being able to develop your ideas and support them with evidence are important skills. When you write an essay, give a speech, or even ask for more allowance, you need to be able to say clearly what your idea is and why you think it's reasonable.

Listen and respond to others' ideas. Even if your first idea about a story is a good one, listening to other people's ideas can help you better understand what you think. You may find new ways to support your idea, or you may change your mind. This will help you with many things in life, like deciding what sports team to join or who to vote for in an election.

Respect other people's points of view. In Junior Great Books, you've seen that two people can read the same story and have different ideas about it without one person having to be wrong. You have also learned to agree and disagree with others politely. These skills will help you get along with others in all parts of your life.

GLOSSARY

In this glossary, you'll find definitions for words that you may not know but are in the stories you've read. You'll find the meaning of each word as it is used in the story. The word may have other meanings as well, which you can find in a dictionary if you're interested. If you don't find a word here that you are wondering about, go to your dictionary for help.

abuse: Bad or mean language meant to insult someone. *The angry man shouted **abuse** at the bus driver who wouldn't let him board.* **Abuse** also means very bad treatment of someone or something. *After years of **abuse**, the jungle gym finally fell apart.*

accustomed: If you are **accustomed** to something, you are used to it. *If you are on a sports team, you grow **accustomed** to having after-school practice every week.*

affront: An insult that is meant to hurt someone's feelings or pride. *It was an **affront** to the honest boy when the manager accused him of stealing.*

agates: An **agate** is a kind of stone that is striped with different colors. ***Agates** are a type of quartz, which is one of the most common minerals found on earth.*

algae: A life form, found mostly in water, that does not have true roots, stems, or leaves like plants do. *Seaweed is a type of **algae**.*

appeal: When something **appeals** to you, you are interested in it. *She felt so sick that even her favorite foods didn't **appeal** to her.*

attentively: Paying close attention. *The children watched the magician **attentively** to try to figure out his tricks.*

barrel organ: A large music box that plays a song when you turn the handle.

battens: Thin strips of wood.

bit: The metal bar on a bridle that fits into a horse's mouth. *The **bit** is attached to the reins, so that when you pull them, the horse stops.*

bluff: A steep, tall cliff or bank. *The climbers went to the top of the **bluff** so they could look down at the ocean.*

bolted: To **bolt** is to run or move suddenly. *When my brother saw his papers blowing away, he **bolted** after them.*

boor: A person with clumsy or rude manners.

brooding: Worrying or thinking very seriously about something for a long time. *It is no use **brooding** over a problem you cannot solve.*

buck up: A phrase that means "cheer up" or "don't be discouraged."

bumps: A tradition in which someone celebrating a birthday is tossed into the air by a group of people, once for every year of the person's age.

burrowing: To **burrow** is to make a hole or a tunnel through something by digging. *The arctic fox was **burrowing** into the snow to keep warm.*

capers: A **caper** is a playful jump or leap. *The puppy was doing **capers** around my feet, wanting me to throw the ball.*

chapatis: A **chapati** is a kind of flat, round bread made of flour, water, and salt. ***Chapatis** are from northern India.*

characters: Written or printed letters or symbols. *It was so dark it was hard to read the **characters** on the sign.*

charged: To **charge** someone to do something is to order or direct that person to do it. *We were **charged** with the job of cleaning our rooms before playing outside.*

chit: A sassy girl or young woman.

civil, civilly: If you are **civil**, you are polite and well-behaved. *I waited **civilly** in line even though others were pushing to get ahead.*

common: As a noun, a **common** is a piece of land shared by a community or group. *All the farmers in town let their sheep graze on the **common**.* As an adjective, to be **common** is to have no special rank or position, or to be usual or regular. *In countries with kings and queens, those who are not in the royal family are **common**. It is **common** to see monkeys in a jungle.*

commotion: Noisy, excited confusion. *There might be **commotion** in the cafeteria if someone starts a food fight.*

compassion: If you have **compassion**, you have a deep understanding of the pain of others and you want to help make that pain go away. *When I was on crutches, my friend showed **compassion** by always slowing down to walk with me. The children felt such **compassion** for the baby bird they found that they made it a nest in a shoebox.*

confidences: Private matters.

consenting: If you **consent** to something, you give permission for it or agree to it. *We ran to buy tickets to the amusement park as soon as we heard our mother **consenting** to let us go.*

cove: A small, sheltered area of water along the shoreline of a larger body of water.

crisps: A British word for "potato chips."

cultivating: Taking care of something—usually a crop of plants—so that it grows. *The farmers are **cultivating** strawberries to sell at the market.*

daft: Foolish or crazy. *You would be **daft** to run across a busy street without looking both ways for cars.*

dazzling: Something **dazzling** is very bright, almost blinding. *The sunlight was so **dazzling** that we had to put on our sunglasses.* **Dazzling** can also mean amazing. *The audience cheered at the circus performer's **dazzling** tricks.*

deftly: Quickly and skillfully. *The expert magician juggled the balls **deftly**.*

dejectedly: When you do something **dejectedly**, you do it in a very sad way or with low spirits. *After looking for her missing dog for hours, the girl walked **dejectedly** home.*

deliberately: When you do something **deliberately**, you do it on purpose. *My mom thinks I broke the plate **deliberately** even though it was really an accident.* **Deliberately** also means with careful thought. *He stepped across the icy street **deliberately** to avoid falling.*

deputy head: The vice principal of a British school.

desperation: When you feel **desperation**, you feel hopeless, sad, or afraid. *With only a few minutes left to finish the test, the boy scribbled some answers out of* ***desperation****.* When something **drives you to desperation**, it makes you feel completely hopeless. *The townspeople had no food or water for weeks and it was* ***driving them to desperation****.*

destination: The place that someone or something is going to. *We were in the car so long I thought we were never going to reach our* ***destination****.*

diesel: A kind of engine fuel that some vehicles use instead of gasoline.

disdain: A feeling of strong dislike or scorn, often felt for someone or something you don't respect. *She rolled her eyes in* ***disdain*** *at the man's rude behavior.*

dispersing, dispersed: To **disperse** is to move apart or scatter in different directions. *At the end of the play, the crowd kept* ***dispersing*** *until the theater was empty. A strong wind* ***dispersed*** *the dandelion's seeds across the lawn.*

dispirited: Something or someone **dispirited** has low energy or is discouraged, and might look tired or sad. *We grew* ***dispirited*** *when a thunderstorm started during our soccer game. Without a breeze, the flag hung down in a* ***dispirited*** *way.*

dreary: When something is **dreary**, it is gloomy or boring. *We don't mind staying inside on a rainy,* ***dreary*** *day. Eating the same lunch every day at school is starting to get* ***dreary****.*

dryly: When you say something **dryly**, you say it in a quietly humorous way, without a lot of emotion. *Our teacher told jokes so* ***dryly*** *that sometimes we did not know when he was kidding.*

elated: If you are **elated**, you are very excited and very happy about something. *I was **elated** when my soccer team won the championship.*

embers: The hot pieces of coal or wood that are left glowing when a fire burns out.

emboldened: If you are **emboldened**, you become bold or encouraged. *The nervous athlete was **emboldened** by the sound of the cheering crowd.*

exasperated: Feeling fed up and annoyed. *I get **exasperated** when they play the same songs over and over on the radio.*

famine: A great lack of food. *During a **famine**, people may starve because they don't have enough to eat.*

farthing: A coin used in the past in Great Britain, equal to one-fourth of a penny.

flung: To **fling** something is to throw or toss it with force. *The baby broke his rattle when he **flung** it onto the floor. She **flung** herself angrily onto her bed and began to cry.*

frail: Weak. *After his long illness, the boy was **frail** and got tired easily.*

frenzy: A state of wild or nervous excitement. *The little boy ran around the room in a **frenzy** when he got his new bike. The cook was in a **frenzy** trying to finish cooking the huge meal by herself.*

gape: To stare at something with your mouth open, usually in wonder or confusion. *As the acrobat walked on the tightrope, we could only stand and **gape**.*

gaudy: Something **gaudy** is very bright or colorful in a way that shows bad taste. *The **gaudy** shoes were covered with too many fake jewels and glitter.*

gaunt: A person who is **gaunt** is very thin or bony.

gewgaws: Small objects without much use that may be kept because they are pretty or fancy. *My grandma has a collection of glass figures and other* ***gewgaws****.*

girths: A **girth** is a strap that goes around a horse's middle to hold a load or saddle on its back. ***Girths*** *are usually made of leather or another very strong material.*

glint: A flash of light.

good riddance: A phrase you use when you are glad that something or someone you don't like is going away or going out of your sight. *My loud, rude neighbors are moving, so* ***good riddance*** *to them!*

granary: A building for storing grain.

gravely: When you do something **gravely**, you do it in a very serious way. *The man listened* ***gravely*** *to the news of the car accident.*

grieve, grieving: To **grieve** is to feel great sadness. *The whole community was* ***grieving*** *after the building burned down.*

grindstones: Large, round stones used to crush grain into flour. *A* ***grindstone*** *can also be used to sharpen or shape tools.*

hearth: A fireplace.

heaved a sigh: To **heave a sigh** is to let it out. *He* ***heaved a sigh*** *of relief when he found his lost keys in his bag.*

heed: To **heed** something is to pay close attention to it. *If you do not* ***heed*** *directions when you're in a strange place, you might get lost.*

hips: The **hip** is the part of a rose that holds the seeds.

hobbled: To **hobble** means to limp or walk stiffly, usually from pain. *The girl with the broken leg* ***hobbled*** *to school on her crutches each day.*

humanity: All people in the world, or the human race. *The basic needs of* ***humanity*** *are food, water, and shelter.* **Humanity** is also the quality of being kind and caring. *She showed great* ***humanity*** *when she helped the homeless man find a place to stay.*

humbly: When you do something **humbly**, you do it with respect or without pride. *The soldiers* ***humbly*** *saluted the president as he walked by them. The winning team* ***humbly*** *accepted the trophy without bragging.*

indignation: If you feel **indignation**, you are upset and angry because you believe that something is unfair. *You might stomp off to your room with* ***indignation*** *if your parents punished you for something you didn't do.*

intentions: Your **intentions** are things you plan to do, or mean to do. *My family's* ***intentions*** *this year are to buy a new house and get a dog. I was late to school again even though my* ***intention*** *was not to be tardy all year.*

jeering: To **jeer** is to make fun of someone or say mean things to them in a rude way. *Nobody could hear the man's speech because the crowd was* ***jeering*** *so loudly.*

joint, jointly: If two or more people own something together, they are **joint** owners of that thing. To do, own, or make something **jointly** means to do it with two or more people. *My cousin and I* ***jointly*** *run our dog walking business.*

kimonos: A **kimono** is a long, loose Japanese robe with wide sleeves and a wide belt. ***Kimonos*** *often have beautiful designs or decorations on them.*

kindling: Small, thin pieces of wood used for starting a fire.

lagged: To **lag** is to fall behind or to be unable to keep up. *I* ***lagged*** *behind the rest of the runners in the race because I was so tired.*

lashed: To **lash** is to speak sharply and angrily at someone. Most often, the word is used with "out" in the phrase **lash out**. *The cashier was shocked when the customer* ***lashed*** *out at him for giving her the wrong change.*

literally: Really or actually. *The children* ***literally*** *jumped for joy when they heard they had a snow day.* If you take something **literally**, you believe exactly what is being said. *When my father said it was raining cats and dogs, my little cousin took it* ***literally*** *and asked to see the animals.*

lolling: To **loll** is to hang loosely. *We realized he was asleep when we saw his head* ***lolling*** *to the side.*

make a fine mock: When you **make a fine mock** of someone, you meanly make fun of that person. *He was worried about wearing his Halloween costume to school because he thought his classmates might* ***make a fine mock*** *of him.*

mangy: Dirty or worn out. *The cat that lives in the alley has* ***mangy*** *fur and a cut on one ear.*

mar: To **mar** something means to damage or spoil it. *You might* ***mar*** *a pair of glasses by scratching one of the lenses.*

mark: In this story, "**mark** you" is an old-fashioned way of saying "pay attention."

marveled: You **marvel** at something that fills you with wonder and surprise. *He **marveled** at how large and deep the Grand Canyon was when he saw it in person.*

***maziwa lala*:** A Swahili phrase for a type of thick milk that tastes somewhat sour.

meditated: To **meditate** is to calm or clear your mind, usually by concentrating on a single thing or thinking quietly. *The woman **meditated** every morning by paying attention to her breathing while she walked through the park.*

meekly: When you do something **meekly**, you do it in a gentle, quiet way or in an obedient way. *She spoke so **meekly** that it was hard for her to get anyone's attention. The servant **meekly** followed every one of the king's orders.*

melancholy: Sad and gloomy. *You might feel **melancholy** if your best friend moved away.*

menacingly: To do something **menacingly** means to do it in a threatening way. *The storm clouds moved in so **menacingly** that the teacher decided to move the class picnic indoors.*

mercy: If you show **mercy**, you treat others with kindness, even though they may not deserve it. *Your parents might show **mercy** by not grounding you after you did something wrong.*

mickle: An old-fashioned Scottish word for "great" or "very large."

millet: Small seeds that come from a type of grass grown in warm countries. ***Millet** is often used to make flour or beer.*

miscellaneous: Made up of different items or parts. *Sock drawers usually contain some **miscellaneous** unmatched socks. I have a box under my bed where I keep **miscellaneous** things like buttons, rocks, and shells.*

mock: In *The Enchanted Sticks,* something that is **mock** is pretend. *The candidates for student council had a **mock** debate before the real one.*

mortar: Usually made of cement, sand, and water, **mortar** is used to hold bricks or stones in place because it gets very hard when it dries.

mourning: The way in which people show sadness that someone has died. *In many countries, you can tell someone is in **mourning** when they wear black clothes.*

murram: A type of clay used for the surface of roads in parts of Africa.

muzzled: A **muzzle** is the long front part of some animals' faces (like horses or dogs), including the nose and mouth. In *The Prince and the Goose Girl,* **muzzled** means pushed or rubbed gently with the nose.

obstinate: Stubborn. ***Obstinate** people will not change their minds about something, no matter how much you argue with them.*

offend: To **offend** someone is to make that person feel insulted or hurt. *My classmate's rude jokes always **offend** me. If you left a party without saying goodbye, you might **offend** the host.*

opal: A precious stone that shows many different colors when placed in the light.

opaque: Something **opaque** is clouded or does not let light pass through it. *You can see through colored balloons but not through **opaque** silver ones.*

osier: A kind of willow tree whose branches are used to make baskets and furniture.

outing: A short trip taken for fun. *During their weekly **outing**, the family had a picnic at the park.*

page: In the Middle Ages, a boy training for knighthood or serving as a nobleman's assistant.

parchment: Animal skin that has been specially prepared so that people can write on it. *In the middle ages, people wrote on **parchment** because paper was much harder to get than it is today.*

pension: Money that is regularly paid to someone after he or she has retired. *After many years of hard work, my grandfather now lives on a monthly **pension**.*

perplexed: Puzzled or confused. *After losing the instructions, he was **perplexed** about how to put together the model airplane.*

plaiting: To **plait** something is to braid it. *We watched the owner of the carpet shop **plaiting** a traditional rug.*

poll: The top of the head.

pounds: British units of money.

protest: A **protest** is a complaint or argument about something that bothers or upsets you. *The crowd shouted in **protest** when the referee ruled against the home team.*

prowling: To **prowl** is to move secretly or quietly, like an animal hunting its prey. *The cat was **prowling** in the yard, looking for birds to chase.*

queue: A British word for a line (the kind you wait in).

railing: To **rail** is to scold or complain in an angry or nasty way. *Our neighbor stood on the porch, **railing** at the children who had broken her window.*

raiment: Clothing.

ravaged: Something that's been **ravaged** has been almost completely destroyed. *The farmer's field of corn was **ravaged** by insects and there was very little left to harvest.*

regain: To **regain** something is to get it back after losing it. *The hiker was able to **regain** his balance after slipping on the loose rocks.*

register: A **register** is a book in which official lists are kept. *Teachers sometimes use a **register** to list the students in class and keep track of how many days they have been absent.*

remarks: A **remark** is a comment. *The guests made many nice **remarks** about the decorations at the party.*

remote: Far away or hidden away. *The **remote** cabin in the woods is miles away from town.*

reticent: If you are **reticent**, you are quiet and prefer to keep your thoughts and feelings to yourself. *The **reticent** girl disliked speaking in class.*

rummage: To **rummage** is to look for something by moving things around in a messy or careless way. *After you **rummage** through your closet looking for your shoes, you might have to put everything back neatly.*

samisen: A Japanese musical instrument with a long neck and three strings.

samurai: A Japanese warrior in the Middle Ages.

savagely: In a dangerous, violent, or fierce way. *The angry dog glared at me **savagely** when I tried to go near him.*

scraggy: Something or someone **scraggy** is skinny or bony. *A stray animal might be **scraggy** if it hasn't eaten for a long time.*

sheepishly: When you do something **sheepishly**, you do it in a way that shows you feel foolish or embarrassed. *After I slipped on a banana peel in front of everyone, I got up **sheepishly**.*

shorn: When something is **shorn**, it is shaved down or cut short. **Shorn** is the past tense of *shear*. *When sheep are **shorn**, their wool is removed to make yarn and other products.*

sinister: Evil or threatening. *The witch in the movie had a **sinister** laugh that made us shiver.*

skeins: A **skein** is a length of yarn or thread loosely twisted in a coil.

slash: When you **slash** something, you cut it with a violent movement, usually with a sharp object. *The chef **slashed** the watermelon in half with a huge knife. I had to keep **slashing** at the tall weeds as I made my way across the overgrown yard.*

slinking: To **slink** is to move in a quiet, sneaky way. *The cat is **slinking** through the grass, trying to catch a mouse.*

smote: Hit with a heavy blow. **Smote** is the past tense of *smite*. *The knight **smote** the dragon with his sword, but it barely made a scratch.*

solemnly: When you do something **solemnly**, you do it very seriously or sincerely. *You might **solemnly** promise never to lie to your best friend. We **solemnly** listened to the lifeguard as she told us how to stay safe while swimming in the ocean.*

solitary: Something or someone **solitary** is alone or likes to be alone. *Owls are **solitary** creatures—once they leave the nest they hunt alone.*

splayed: To **splay** something is to spread it out or spread it apart. *The tired boy rested on the ground with his legs **splayed** in front of him.*

sponsored: An event that is **sponsored** is paid for by someone else, often because the event is for a good cause or for charity. *The money raised by the **sponsored** race was donated to the animal shelter.*

squarely: Directly. *She hit the nail **squarely** on the head with the hammer.*

stanch: To stop liquid from flowing. *You can sometimes **stanch** a bloody nose by pinching your nose shut.*

start: A **start** is a quick, surprised movement. *I gave a **start** when my friend snuck up behind me and tapped my shoulder.*

strewn: Scattered or spread all over. *Flowers were **strewn** on the path where the bride was walking.*

strides: A **stride** is a very long step. *My mother takes such big **strides** that she was always able to catch me quickly when I was a toddler.*

structure: Something that has been built. *A **structure** might be a house, a bridge, or a dam.*

stumping: To **stump** is to walk in a clumsy, heavy way. *The elephant went **stumping** through the jungle, smashing plants under its feet.*

stunned: When you are **stunned**, you are so surprised you don't know what to say or do. *We were so **stunned** that we'd won the contest that we just stared at one another.*

surplus: More of something than you need or can use.

surrender: To **surrender** is to give up or admit to losing. *The battle went on and on until the weaker army finally had to **surrender**.*

suspicion: When you have a **suspicion**, you have a feeling about something (especially something wrong or bad) but you don't know for certain. *I had a **suspicion** that the man had stolen something when I saw him run quickly out of the store.*

swagger: To walk in a bold, proud way. *You might **swagger** across the field after your team wins a soccer match.*

swerved: To **swerve** is to turn aside or change direction very suddenly, often to avoid hitting something. *The driver **swerved** around the fallen tree branch.*

sympathy: A feeling of understanding for someone else's troubles or sorrow. *When the principal's car was stolen, everyone felt great **sympathy** for him.*

talons: The claws of a bird of prey, such as an owl or a hawk.

taunt: To **taunt** is to try to upset someone by teasing or making fun of that person. *You might **taunt** your little sister by holding her favorite toy just out of her reach.*

tempted: When you're **tempted** by something, you want to do it or to have it very much, even if it's wrong or foolish. *He was **tempted** to open the gift he found in the closet, even though his birthday was still a week away.*

thrashing: To **thrash** is to move violently or wildly. *I knew my brother was having a nightmare when I saw him **thrashing** in his bed.*

throng: A large group of people gathered closely together. *The **throng** of kids on the playground was making a lot of noise.*

thronged: To **throng** is to crowd or move closely together. *A large group of fans **thronged** on the sidewalk after the baseball game.*

till: A cash register.

tracking: To **track** is to follow the trail of an animal or person. *When you are **tracking** an animal, you try to figure out which way it went by looking for signs such as footprints or droppings.*

trifles: A **trifle** is something that has little value or importance. *All the class spelling bees I ever competed in seem like **trifles** compared to the national bee.*

trilled: To **trill** is to make a high-pitched musical hum. *The birds outside **trilled** loudly and woke us up.*

trothed: Two people who are **trothed** have made a promise to marry each other.

troupe: A group. *A **troupe** of singers, dancers, and actors often travel and work together.*

***uganga*:** A Swahili word for a type of magic.

untrustworthy: Not honest or reliable. *You might decide your sister is **untrustworthy** if she keeps taking things from your room and lying about it.*

vicious: Something or someone **vicious** is mean and fierce and might try to hurt others. *The **vicious** dog barked and growled before it attacked. The **vicious** bully picks fights every day.*

wager: To **wager** is to bet. *I'll **wager** five dollars that you can't eat that whole pie.*

wallowed: When you **wallow** in something, you get completely caught up in it or you take a little too much pleasure in it. *My sister **wallowed** in sadness when her favorite singer got married.* To **wallow** can also mean to roll around in something with enjoyment. *The pigs grunted with pleasure as they **wallowed** in the mud.*

wantonly: In a cruel and uncaring manner. *Some badly behaved students **wantonly** crushed the flowers that had just been planted in front of the library.*

withdrawn: If you are **withdrawn**, you are lost in thought, or you do not like to talk to others very much. *After arguing with my friend, I became **withdrawn**, thinking about everything we had said. The **withdrawn** girl sat quietly by herself at the party.*

woe: Great sorrow or suffering.

wry: To be **wry** means to be funny in a quiet or teasing way, sometimes without much emotion. *He has a **wry** sense of humor and not everyone understands his jokes.* When you make a **wry** expression, you twist your face to show you are displeased or annoyed.

ACKNOWLEDGMENTS

All possible care has been taken to trace ownership and secure permission for each selection in this series. The Great Books Foundation wishes to thank the following authors, publishers, and representatives for permission to reproduce copyrighted material:

Kamau's Finish, by Muthoni Muchemi, from MEMORIES OF SUN, edited by Jane Kurtz. Copyright © 2002 by Muthoni Muchemi. Reproduced by permission of the author.

Ghost Cat, from EERIE ANIMALS: SEVEN STORIES, by Donna Hill. Copyright © 1983 by Donna Hill. Reproduced by permission of Margery Smith.

The Hemulen Who Loved Silence, from TALES FROM MOOMINVALLEY, by Tove Jansson. Copyright © 1962 by Tove Jansson. Reproduced by permission of Farrar, Straus, and Giroux, LLC.

THE ENCHANTED STICKS, by Steven J. Myers. Copyright © 1979 by Steven J. Myers. Reproduced by permission of the author.

Kaddo's Wall, from THE COW-TAIL SWITCH AND OTHER WEST AFRICAN STORIES, by Harold Courlander and George Herzog. Copyright © 1947, 1975 by Harold Courlander. Reproduced by permission of Henry Holt and Company, LLC.

A Bad Road for Cats, from EVERY LIVING THING, by Cynthia Rylant. Copyright © 1985 by Cynthia Rylant. Reproduced by permission of Atheneum Books for Young Readers, an imprint of Simon & Schuster Children's Publishing.

Lenny's Red-Letter Day, from I'M TRYING TO TELL YOU, by Bernard Ashley. Copyright © 1981 by Bernard Ashley. Reproduced by permission of the author.

THROUGH THE MICKLE WOODS, by Valiska Gregory. Copyright © 1992 by Valiska Gregory. Reproduced by permission of Adams Literary as agents for the author.

ILLUSTRATION CREDITS

Illustrations for *Kamau's Finish* copyright © 2014 by Colin Bootman.

Illustrations for *Ghost Cat* copyright © 2014 by David Johnson.

Illustrations for *The Hemulen Who Loved Silence* copyright © 1962 by Tove Jansson. Reproduced by permission of Farrar, Straus, and Giroux, LLC.

Illustrations for *The Enchanted Sticks* copyright © 2014 by Bagram Ibatoulline.

Illustrations for *Kaddo's Wall* copyright © 2014 by Brian Pinkney.

Illustrations for *The Prince and the Goose Girl* and *Through the Mickle Woods* copyright © 2014 by Helen Cann.

Illustrations for *A Bad Road for Cats* copyright © 2014 by Wendy Hogue Berry.

Illustrations for *Lenny's Red-Letter Day* copyright © 2014 by Hajra Meeks.

Cover art copyright © 2014 by Liz Cleaves.

Design by THINK Book Works.